"Magical and original, *Laketown* is filled with tales that open the mind and heart to feelings of longing and wonderment."
— Nancy Rae Stone, producer: *Air Force One, Spy Game, The Family Man,* etc.

"Soulful and romantic, *Laketown* instills a sense of peace, even as bold and magical events are happening before you."
— Jon Turtletaub, producer and director: *Cool Runnings, The Meg, Phenomenon, While You Were Sleeping,* etc.

"With a touch of the metaphysical and an inspired imagination, DiPego takes us on a great ride."
— Michael Taylor, film and TV producer, professor of USC School of Cinematic Arts

"The read was fascinating. Highly recommended!"
— Elayne Klasson, author of *Love Is a Rebellious Bird*

"In these stories, the genuine brilliance and full delight of a natural-born, finely-honed storyteller are on display."
— Ron Colone, author, essayist, and writer/columnist for California Central Coast newspapers; Artist Advocacy Foundation Director

Laketown

Also by Gerald DiPego

NOVELS
Cheevey
Keeper of the City
With a Vengeance

NONFICTION
Write! Find the Truth in Your Fiction

SCREENPLAYS
Phenomenon
Message in a Bottle
Sharky's Machine
The Forgotten
Angel Eyes
Instinct
Words and Pictures

STAGE PLAYS AND FILMS FOR TELEVISION
154 and Paradise
I Heard the Owl Call My Name
A Family Upside Down

Laketown

a novel in stories

Gerald DiPego

IDLEWILD PUBLISHING · SANTA YNEZ, CA · 2024

ISBN: 979-8-9891227-0-7

Idlewild Publishing
Post Office Box 1329
Santa Ynez, CA 93460

To my cousin Carolyn St. Pe,
who saw me as a writer when I was twelve,
and never stopped believing

Acknowledgments

Thank you to my loving wife, Chris, for her confidence and joy in her husband's trade, and to my Author Assistant Christine Beebe for her wisdom and wit, and to my fine sons, Justin and Zachary, from whom I am constantly learning.

Contents

Preface

I was raised in a northern Illinois lake town. I walked to school through a farmer's field and bicycled along gravel roads to work at our small "Tip Top Food Mart," opened by my father who immigrated from Italy at the age of nineteen.

I was captured early in life by stories. I read Tarzan books and works by Jules Verne and Robert Louis Stevenson, and was captivated by films on television. Gobbling up stories of all kinds, I asked myself, "Could I do that? Could I *make* a story?"

On weekends I fished in the channel leading to the lake, sometimes catching bluegill and now and then a larger carp, enjoying the battle, and if I won, gave it to a neighbor who knew how to prepare that bottom-feeding fish. All the while I carried stories in my head, making them up, shaping them, collecting them like coins I would spend one day. The stories in this book are built of fiction, but the town where they take place is built of memory as clear as the lake itself.

—Jerry

Laketown

The Man with Three Fists

T HE MAN WITH THREE FISTS was Hank Wenslow, and all
of this happened in the lake towns of northeastern Illinois
in the 1950's. In fact, it was probably 1954 in Chicago, but in
the small towns of Lake County it was still 1951 or '52 because
life was slower and smaller there.

Wenslow was a farmer, and the problem was a shortage of
rain. If you check the records for a particularly dry spring and
summer, you won't find it, because that same May and June
it rained heavily in Fox Lake, Grays Lake, Round Lake and
Wonder Lake, and a chain of storms drenched Pistakee Bay,
but in the village of Indian Lake, where Wenslow raised corn,
it didn't even drizzle.

The tall farmer could be found walking every day between
his rows of the still-green corn, his boots raising a light dust, and
the emerging stalks beginning to fade and crack, and every time

he saw a crack, thin as a razor cut, it hurt him in his own flesh. He walked his fields even at night in that season, and his wife watched him from the farmhouse when the moon was bright, but she didn't know that whenever he brought his hand to his mouth, he was weeping.

He hadn't wept since the war had marched him through Italy and Germany, since the constant shelling had cracked him like a dry stalk, and he had cried for two days and nights, and then soldiered on. He was weeping now because he couldn't help his corn, couldn't protect it, and it would likely die. It wasn't that he would lose the farm from one bad season. It was for the corn itself that he wept, for its suffering and for its fragility, and this sorrow and anxiety congealed in his stomach into a knot of pain the size and weight of a big man's fist, and that's how he came to imagine it: a fist clenched hard in his gut, the skin tight and the knuckles white, and it diminished his appetite and stole his sleep and moved him by inches toward a desperation that was next door to madness.

People liked Wenslow well enough and respected him for his hard work and his dependability, and they liked his wife, too, with the qualification that Sandra was a strange one, a strange kinda girl, they would say, though at this time the Wenslows were over thirty, and thirty then carried the weight of forty now.

They were a quiet couple even when young, then further muffled by the tragedy of a child born too early and alive for only three weeks. They had no other children, and no family closer than Moline.

Wenslow had his corn, and Sandra had her feral cats and

the birds that nested near the house and in the barn. She hired young boys to come with their air rifles one summer because the starlings had arrived and were attacking all her other birds, and those two neighbor boys made a pile of five dead starlings to show her, but she walked by them and drew in her breath and then came down softly on her knees in the barnyard to stare at a bird lying alone, and she said only, "It's my purple martin," but she said it with enough weight of sorrow to crush those boys for a week. They never saw her weep, but only stare at the splayed wings and the dead little eye, and it was likely she saw her tiny, withered child in that bird, and likely too that Wenslow saw the little boy's ghost in every dying stalk of corn.

The local farmers and builders and even some of the factory workers who came home every night on the train from Chicago would stop in at the Lake Bar near the station and have a beer or a whiskey, and it was over a shot of Seagram's Seven one hot early evening that Wenslow met Albingo. He wasn't much older than Wenslow, but with ancient eyes that studied the tall farmer who was alone at a table. Wenslow sought solitude that summer, not company, and the others were glad to avoid him because his deep silences rang like a great bell that filled the room, and his weariness and sorrow blurred his face.

Wenslow sat in a corner staring at his hand and clenching that hand into a tight fist and then slowly releasing it. Carl Fanucci, a dusty contractor at the bar, said to his brother, "Looks like Hank Wenslow hurt his hand," and his brother Johnny, a roofer, stared and nodded.

"Yep. Keeps favoring it. Maybe he's got arthritis."

But Carl said, "Nahh, he's too young for arthritis, ain't he?"

Wenslow did not have arthritis. He was only trying, again and again, to loosen the knot in his gut, to imagine it like a fist that was giving up its grip and opening slowly, like a sigh.

Wenslow may have felt the stares of the Fanuccis somehow, because he looked up from his hand, and the men quickly looked away, but in the bar's mirror he saw the stare of another man, and this time it was Wenslow who looked away, hoping the man, Irv Kiner, a teacher at the high school, would not come over to talk. Irv might do that, if he had had more than two drinks. Three drinks would make the man come and sit with Wenslow and talk about what they shared, what they did not speak of to anyone else. They had both fought in Italy, both at Anzio, pinned down and then finally moving up the boot, town by town, and Wenslow talked to no one else about the war, because what good did it do to remember? It was all stashed and locked in his mind and why open it? Irv Kiner would talk till his eyes teared, and he would tell his stories, which Wenslow knew by now, and Wenslow hoped Irv would not come to his table, and he hoped the man would find his own box and drop his stories in there and turn the goddamn lock. But it was not Irv who left the bar and came over to him. It was Albingo, walking toward him without any rush, but with a purpose.

The smaller man had been in the area for ten days, looking for work, clearing brush and telling people he was an Indian from Mexico, prominent in his tribe, but later it was said he was a Spanish Gypsy, and this is likely because the Gypsies came through the lake towns in those days in their trailers and made and sold lawn furniture from their camps every summer. The Indian Lake children would glance at the Gypsy camp as they rode by on their bikes, snatching a look into what they imagined was an exotic and fearful world, as if they were riding past encamped Apaches or Chinese bandits, but they saw only old trailers and trucks and families and lawn furniture.

"You have a farm, they say."

Wenslow looked up from his hand, and Albingo sat down uninvited, but he had brought his beer from the bar and a glass of Seagram's for Wenslow which he placed very close to the thick, roughened hand that was in half-clench now and still. Wenslow stared a moment at the whiskey before he looked at Albingo and nodded a silent thanks.

"You have work for me?"

This time, within Wenslow's long pause, Albingo raised his beer and clinked the bottle softly against the farmer's glass. Wenslow picked up the whiskey and they drank, each man closing his eyes for one second in unconscious ritual.

"No more brush," Albingo said. "I have the poison ivy." Here he turned his hands, laying his knuckles on the table, showing his inner arms, from elbows to wrists, covered in small blisters.

Wenslow gave this another nod and then said, "I've got no work now. Sorry." He returned his eyes to the tabletop and then to his hand, and he tried once more, clenching it tightly and releasing it, hoping to feel the release in his stomach, but feeling only the warmth of the whiskey and the same fierce knot inside.

Albingo watched this, his chin in his hand, and he said, "You have the three fists."

Wenslow jolted in his chair, but it was a quiet jolt, and nobody seemed to notice. He stared hard at Albingo as the man, tired from his work and relaxed by the beer, went on. "It's what my people say, the Indians: 'Two fists for work and one inside for worry. *Tres puños.*' I work for five dollars a day and food, okay?"

The farmer pushed his stare deep into the dark and ancient eyes. The smaller man only shrugged. "I do all kinds of work. What do you need?"

"Rain." The word was out of Wenslow before he knew he was saying it, and it caused, in Albingo, a fit of slow nodding.

"What have you got? The alfalfa?"

"I've got corn."

Albingo nodded for another long while and then finished his beer. "Muscatel," he said. "You like the wine?" Wenslow had never tasted muscatel. He had never tasted a great many things.

Albingo stood up slowly. He had had three beers. He said "Muscatel" again, as if confirming an opinion. "Then you show me."

"Show you what?"

"Your corn."

—·—

SANDRA Wenslow watched at the windows for her husband to come home. In any other season two hours late could mean an accident, but in this unblessed summer, she had seen her man changing with every dry week, drooping and fading as his corn faded, and she knew he was out there somewhere within his long straight rows of dying soldiers.

She wrapped his dinner in aluminum foil. She watched half of a television program they would have watched together. She visited every window in her home as if they were stations of the cross, looking for his truck and hoping against another dying.

—·—

WENSLOW sat with Albingo in the darkness at the edge of his field where the spread of his corn topped a low hill, and he knew as he leaned back into the cracking weeds that the chiggers were biting him and he would itch for a week, but he was in the grip of a desperate hope and stayed where he was, his mind keeping at bay the insect bites and the images of Sandra alone in the house with only the thought of him, like a ghost, sitting beside her and watching their programs together and sometimes, when the very funniest thing was said, turning to trade with her his thin twisted smile for her shining one.

His hope came from the way Albingo had looked at his corn and touched it and pondered and sipped the muscatel and passed to Wenslow the bottle of sweet wine and the lore of his ancient people, the Aztecs.

"It's not possible to rain all around here, my friend, all around, but not here," he said with certainty, "unless there's a curse."

"Jesus," Wenslow said, and Albingo nodded gravely.

"But there are ways," he added, "to fight the curses." He

drained the last of the wine and threw the bottle out over the corn like a benediction. They heard it ring and roll on the hard ground. "Look," he said, and he lay back fully in the weeds beside Wenslow, staring straight up, and the farmer followed his stare. No more was said until the full moon claimed its height and put out nearly every star, and by then Wenslow, hearing Albingo's slow and steady breathing, was certain the man was asleep, while he himself also lay back and looked above at nothing with wide, expectant eyes, mosquitoes stinging his forehead and a fist gripping his intestines.

But then Albingo spoke within the rhythm of his even breathing. "You know what the night sky is, Wenslow?"

Wenslow moved his head from side to side, signaling "No" by the rustling of dry weeds.

"She is the mystery of the woman."

Men are always comparing everything to a woman. Speak of a musical instrument, a bottle of wine, a horse; discuss, in a group of men, a tractor, and one of them will compare this to a beautiful woman and tell you why, but Albingo seemed to be calling on wisdom ancient and eternal, and Wenslow was drunk on the mixture of whiskey, sweet wine and desperation, so he listened hard through the shrill beat of the crickets.

"The dark of the night sky is the darkness between the legs of a beautiful woman."

Wenslow pondered this, trying to imagine the vastness of the night as one immense female crotch with black, silken hair. The image made him vaguely uncomfortable. He had never explored that territory with any diligence, feeling in its presence

like an awkward and uneducated stranger. He had touched it
experimentally. He had felt excitement at the sight of it and
tenderness, too, but he had mainly kept his distance, presenting
his loins to it, but not his close inspection. Sandra had never led
him there, and so he had not gone, and when, in their early,
exuberant tumblings, before time and tragedy had slowed and
tamed them, he had found himself in proximity to this mystery,
which, in the case of Sandra, was, in fact, sandy-colored, he
had felt a reverential awe, as if he had strayed too close to the
altar of a church.

"Now," Albingo said, and here he was whispering, which
brought from Wenslow an intense and focused listening.
"Now...see the moon?" It was a full and perfect moon. "The
moon is inside the mystery. Inside. The moon is that place
inside a woman that, if you touch it, she will tremble. You
know? She trembles, and then she cries out, and then, if you
keep touching, she lets go. She lets go her honey. You know?"

Wenslow had heard of this. In the army the map of the
woman was traveled endlessly and covered in encyclopedias
of talk, whole libraries of education, speculation, fantasies and
lies, and he had only half listened because it was mostly a dishonoring, he felt, a dirtying of something pure, something that
he wanted so much to be good and pure, and after returning
home and courting and marrying, he had never mentioned
this to Sandra or asked her any questions, feeling that their
parts were doing what they were supposed to be doing, and it
felt good to him and seemed to feel good to her, and her smile
had shined at him when, early on, the two of them had been

surprised and even a bit embarrassed over the extent of their ecstasy, and the rest, he figured, was none of his business.

So he understood Albingo's words and tried to imagine, in the sky above him, that the blackness was one giant tuft of silky black hair and the moon was one mysterious node within that larger mystery, a place invisible to him until tonight, and as he stared, he saw the moon, for once, not as a shiny circle, but as a ball of flesh, palpable, glowing.

"Reach," Albingo said, lifting his hand slowly toward the sky. "Reach through the hair and the second lips of the woman, and…" Here his hand reformed as his index finger thrust out. "…touch the moon."

Wenslow reached, and, with a fingertip, he covered the round, shining moon, and imagined he was gently touching it.

"Touch it. Touch it." Albingo's finger moved slightly, rhythmically, and so did Wenslow's. "Touch it. Touch it. And then… the rain comes."

"Rain?" Wenslow dropped his hand and sat up quickly, turning to Albingo who was washed white in the moonlight.

The man was slowly bringing his fingertip back from the moon. He put the finger in his mouth, tasted it, closing his eyes for one second, and then he sighed and turned to Wenslow and began to nod. "It's how you make it rain, my people say. You do this to the woman in the sky, in the full moon. Her rain comes."

"What woman? What d'you mean?"

"Her rain blesses the land."

Wenslow shook his head roughly, as if to slosh away the alcohol and said, "Wait, wait. What woman?"

"Woman of the rain. I forget her name. Chali-something. Inca goddess."

"Inca? I thought you said you were Aztec."

"I'm half Inca, half Aztec, like a priest, so I know this. Chali-something is her name."

Wenslow was squinting hard at the man and still slightly shaking his head, trying for clarity. "What d'you mean? What do I do? You mean pray to her?" Wenslow was ready to pray if praying to some goddess beyond the southern border might help his corn.

"No, touch her, make her honey come."

"Who, goddamnit?"

Albingo's eyes were small and dangerously sleepy as he lay beside Wenslow, the beers and the wine tucking him into his bed of weeds. Wenslow suddenly stood over him with all three of his fists tight and trembling. "Who?!"

"I tol' you. There's a curse here."

"Yes! A curse!"

"So she comes—when there's a curse, a drought, they say she comes to the place as a human woman. You find her. You go to her. You make love. You touch her. A real woman, but Chali-something, too. Look for somebody, she's new, and she looks like Chali."

Albingo closed his eyes, and Wenslow moved quicker than thought, putting one of his big fists into Albingo's shirt and lifting him six inches off the ground, causing his eyes to pop open. "What will she look like?!"

Albingo's eyes showed surprise but not fear, and when he

heard the cracking in Wenslow's voice, the desperate, liquid, last-hope cracking, his stare went to deep sadness for this tall farmer, and Wenslow, seeing this sadness, lowered the man gently back into the weeds.

Albingo shrugged in the moonlight. "Somebody new. Somebody…black hair. And the skirt. They call her 'The Woman in the Green Skirt.' It's old, old religion. The religion says she's here now, and you'll find her and love her and touch her, and she'll make the rain, and that's what I know, Wenslow."

The goddess that Albingo was reaching for and certainly dishonoring was Chalchiuhtlicue, a helper of the Aztec rain god Tlāloc, and she is, in truth, known as "The Lady of the Jade Skirt," but in paintings the skirt is blue, and her powers are knit with storms and death by drowning, and maybe Albingo was misremembering or retelling a tale told to him that had been damaged along the way.

Wenslow sat down with his head in his hands, his brain feeling swollen and soggy, and he would have wept with frustration and shame at the wild wreck he had become, ready to believe anything, to clutch at a myth, to clutch at a man's shirt and lift him off the ground in near violence, but his tears were halted, along with his breath, by the rumble of thunder. It was distant, muffled, as if some giant night goddess had turned over in her sleep miles away, but it was, unmistakably, thunder, and then there was the wind. It blew in one long, building gust, westerly across the corn into Wenslow's face, ruffling his hair as he raised his head from his hands and opened his mouth slightly in surprise and drank in the rushing air that tasted of rain. He held his breath as the dark and somehow womanly sky seemed to heave out a long, palpable sigh and then grow quiet.

And in the quiet, Albingo said, "She's waiting for you."

"She's here, then," Wenslow said, "a real woman," willing himself to believe, staring across his moonlit rows of corn. "She came because of the drought, right? And so she's here since… May, maybe, when it dried out."

Albingo said "Mm," his eyes closed, and his body settling into sleep.

"Green dress," Wenslow said to himself. "Black hair, and I'm supposed to… Oh, Jesus." He dropped his head into his hands again. "Find her and then… God." His mission, when placed into the reality of Indian Lake, Illinois, and its streets and trees and people and into the reality of himself, his own awkward, reticent self, his own life, his marriage, his nearly halted sexuality, seemed impossible, but what else could he reach for? He looked at the moon again, its fierce light almost too bright for his eyes. What else was left?

"Pretty soon, my friend." Albingo's voice was more than halfway lost to sleep. "Before the moon gets small."

"What?!"

"Full moon is the time. Maybe…you got a few days." And Albingo was gone, and Wenslow was alone with the waiting goddess above him. He dropped his eyes to the corn and received the strength he needed from the stunted, drying stalks who, in their fragility, asked for his protection.

—·—

Sandra lay in bed in her thin baby-dolls because the night was warm, and when she received the blessing that was the sound of her husband's truck, she sent out a silent thank you like a radio broadcast to whomever was listening, stopping short of mentioning God or picturing angels because she had spent all her religious prayers in the attempt to save her newborn son, and when that had failed, she had given up, not in bitterness, but with the notion that she was somehow unworthy, that her son had come too early because of her, because she wanted him too much and wasn't patient, and the little boy had left them because she wanted so much for him to stay, and now she tried very hard not to want anything very badly, afraid that her intense wanting would somehow kill it. So, even this moment, this pleasure at hearing the sound of Hank's old truck was placed in cotton and muffled like some secret she mustn't show.

She followed each of his heavy steps and then the fall of his boots in the mudroom and his padding through the kitchen and the bumping of a chair and his pause in the bathroom and the closing of that door and the distant sound of his peeing and the flush and the hiss of the water in the sink and the opening of the door and his entrance into the bedroom and the unzipping and falling of his clothes over the chair, and then he was rocking the bed like a boat with his heavy bone and muscle, making his passage toward her, trying to be quiet and ease softly beside her in case she slept, and she was comforted by the gentle connection of his flesh to hers along her back as if a missing piece of herself had been returned and attached, and then she smelled the drink on his breath and this disappointed and worried her, and she felt his sorrow for his aching over the drying, dying corn.

She didn't turn to him, but whispered in the darkness, "I'm awake."

She heard him swallow and breathe and felt the soft landing of his large, rough hand on her bare shoulder, and that comforted her, also, and he asked her, "Did you hear that wind?"

She nodded slightly, and he felt the nodding in the darkness. "Rattled the windows," she said.

"It did?" Wenslow was glad that he hadn't imagined the wind, and he spent a whole minute remembering it, remembering all the words of Albingo, and Sandra thought he was finished speaking to her. She wished he'd say more, but she wouldn't let herself want that too much or he was sure to stop— because of her wanting. "Anything good on tonight?" he asked her.

"Danny Thomas."

She felt his nodding in the darkness and tried to remember the very funniest thing that had happened on the show so she could tell him, and maybe they'd laugh together in a whisper, but she hadn't been concentrating on the program, only waiting and worrying. "Aren't you hungry?" she asked him, and she felt him moving his head and knew he was saying "no." His big calloused hand slid as softly as it could down her bare arm and stopped at her bent elbow and then moved to her hip, to the thin material of her pajamas and rested there, and she felt the warmth of it, but it didn't stay. She hoped it would stay, and that's why it moved on, down the short span of her baby-doll bottoms to touch her bare thigh, and she caught her breath and held it. She didn't want to. She hadn't wanted to in a long while, and she didn't want to now. She was afraid to want to and afraid to do it because she was afraid to find out that she never wanted to do it again. She didn't think he wanted to either, didn't think he wanted her that way anymore because he hadn't touched her like this in so long, and she thought he was just taking care of himself in the shower maybe, and that was enough because look at all the pain, all the pain that had come from it, from their pleasure, and it wasn't worth it, what it had given them and what it had taken away, too much, everything.

Wenslow was not planning to make love to his wife. He didn't have the heart for it and knew she didn't either. He could feel the tension in her body as he laid his hand on her thigh, but he didn't need to feel her fear to know that it was a bad idea. He missed their physical love, and remembered it as a great blessing that had come and gone. Oh, her slim legs, oh, her breasts cupped in his hands, oh, her mouth, their mouths making one mouth, all of it a treasure. When the pregnancy came, he had been so careful with her. They had continued, as her body grew, but he made himself light, keeping his weight off her with his elbows and knees because of that fragile egg in her, the egg of life, and after little Bryan had come and gone, a span of twenty-two days, they had tried several times to find comfort in their sexual love, and he had made himself light again, because there was still an egg in her, the egg of sorrow, and, being empty, this egg was even more fragile, but they had found no comfort, only more pain, and, over time, they had stopped, stopped now for fourteen months, and so, as he stroked her smooth thigh, he felt her fear and wanted to take it away, and so he whispered, "No... No, we won't. I just... We won't. I just..." And with gentle pressure he turned her onto her back.

The moon found the bedroom window and began to look inside by degrees, watching them, making Sandra's baby-dolls glow white and showing where the top had pulled up and bared her stomach, and Wenslow laid his cheek there, on her flesh, keeping his large head light with the muscles of his neck. He was staring down now at her thin, white shorts, her covered crotch and naked thighs, the sheet being around their knees, and he was thinking, in his muddy, drunken brain, about the woman he must find and what he must do to save his dying corn and how this would be a sin, not just a religious sin, but a sin against Sandra, only it wasn't for himself but for all the withering stalks that needed his protection, and shouldn't that absolve him? He moved his hand from her thigh to the elastic of her baby-doll shorts, and he whispered, "We won't. I just..." And he pulled down the shorts to bare her crotch to the moonlight, and he stared at her hair, sparse and sandy there, not at all the night sky, but beautiful, and the memory made him swallow tears that suddenly gathered in his throat. This soft flesh, in front of his face, was the mystery he had to penetrate in order to bring the rain, and he wanted to study it, but the memories of their love-making flooded into his vision and blinded him, and the tears gathered again, and he couldn't swallow them. He placed a light, wet kiss on her skin, and then he began to weep, an almost silent weeping, but she felt it in the slight movement of his head and in the tears that touched her belly, and she sent a hand down slowly to slip into his hair and caress his scalp, and after a moment, he groaned softly and sighed, and his breathing became even, and he fell asleep.

He awoke at seven, an hour late for him, with his head stuffed and aching. Sandra was making breakfast, and he joined her, and last night's touching and weeping was added automatically to the list of things not to be mentioned, along with corn and rain and sex and little Bryan James Wenslow.

By nine-thirty he was at the lumber yard picking up six new fence posts when the contractor, Fanucci, said to him, "Hear about the wreck last night?"

He shook his head, noticing the weight of the younger man's stare, not only sorrow, but a troubled look, as if Carl Fanucci could not make this event, this "wreck" fit into his mind.

"Emily Bridger," Fanucci said. "Just eighteen. Dead at eighteen. Did you know her?"

"No. I heard the name. 'Bridger.'"

"Yeah. Her mom's at the savings and loan. Her father's… well he's got a bad back. I built a garage for 'em. The kid was just around fourteen then. Shy kid. God, it must be rotten when they're so young."

Wenslow nodded, sorry of course, but thinking how easily Fanucci seemed to be forgetting Wenslow's own child. Maybe tiny Bryan James died too soon, and so had not seemed to leave a hole in the town and cause this ripple of sorrow and wonder, like Emily Bridger, like the boy who had drowned in the lake years ago and was still remembered as a caution, while Bryan James was somehow gone from the common memory of the lake towns. Maybe it was more than his being so young. Maybe some of the forgetting came because he was so small, simply too small a package of life, too light to be remembered.

Fanucci shook his head quickly to snap the thought from his brain and went about the loading of his pick-up, saying to Wenslow, "Henning got some rain at his place last night," and Wenslow dropped Emily Bridger from the front of his mind and felt his third fist tighten even more, more than he thought was possible. He almost cried out at the clutch of it, barely able to ask…

"Real rain?"

"Well, some drops. You?"

Wenslow shook his head, and then before Fanucci could turn away, he said, "I hear there's a woman—a woman who came to town in the last couple of months…" He felt stupid saying this as he watched Fanucci's face wrinkle in confusion. He went on, the words limp now. "Dark-haired woman, new in town."

The contractor was squinting and pondering as he filled his truck bed, shaking his head, saying, "What about her?"

And now what? What could he say? It was all so stupid. "Somebody told me. Somebody mentioned her. Maybe…she needs work or something." He shrugged and Fanucci shrugged, and it was over. Wenslow's face was flushed, and he left the lumber yard as soon as he could, even slamming his door, even speeding away, so goddamn angry at himself, at Albingo, at the fist in his gut, at the blue sky picked clean, not a feather of a cloud, not a promise.

He drove to the cluster of shops along Highway 83 that called itself a town and braked at the only stop light in six miles, feeling ashamed that he still held some lingering belief, like the headache that plagued him from the wine, a residue of desperate faith in the Albingo method of bringing rain. "But what if?" he said to himself, shouting it inside his head. "Just what if?" And then he said it aloud, sitting there in the cab of his truck. "What the hell *if!?*" He had to try every "if." He had to. Because the last time there was a life under his protection, he hadn't done everything. He hadn't tried every "if," and he wasn't going to do that again.

Myrna Gresha, whom they barely knew, and who spoke so seldom to him or to anyone, had stopped him on the street with a look that caught and held on and she had said, "Hank Wenslow, you rub that tiny boy with witch hazel every morning and every night. You massage that little early baby," and she had walked on, and he told the doctor, and the doctor had scoffed, and he hadn't done it. Why the hell not? What the hell if? And he hadn't fixed the seal on the storm windows, not perfectly, and what if there had been a draft? And he hadn't prayed enough, and once he threw his hat on the bed without thinking, and he hadn't held his son enough, and he hadn't tried the goddamn witch hazel!

The light changed, and he began to drive on, but then slowed because of a sudden wind, as powerful as the surprising gust that had come last night, and he saw it raising the dust in the ditches of the highway and heard it through his half-open windows and even tasted the grit of it, and turned his head away, and that's when he saw, out of his side window, that the wind was raising the skirt of a woman who had just stepped out of Keanes's Dry Cleaners, and it was showing him the tops of her stockings and a glimpse of bare thighs, and it was flying her long black hair like a flag and puffing the skirt one more time as she batted it down, and that skirt was perfectly green.

His mouth opened and stayed that way, even as the dust powdered his lips and coated his teeth, and he watched the wind leave her skirt and let go of her hair, and he saw her walk on as the last of the gust died away.

He U-turned and got ahead of her and parked the truck and stepped out, checking the sky again, and there they were. Three small clouds had appeared at the rim, just a suggestion of clouds at the western rim. He began to walk across the highway as if he didn't know she was there, but his path would intersect her path, and he was shuffling his mind like a deck of cards, hoping the right words would show up, when she suddenly said, "Now that was a crazy wind. Where did it go? Where does wind go, anyway?"

He looked at her to make sure she was talking to him, but she didn't give him her eyes, moving her head to scout the town and sending her hand into her blown hair. She was a bit older than him, he guessed, and lush in her figure and tall, but light and quick in her step, and when she did turn her face to him, he saw that her eyes were strong and dark and beautiful. She was not exactly hard, but confident and seeming not to give a damn what anybody thought. "Do you know where the wind goes?" she asked him.

"I'm Wenslow," he said. "Hank Wenslow," and he stopped in her path.

She walked around him, saying, "I suppose it just disappears, or does it fly all the way around the world—the wind?"

He caught up to her and had to use his own long stride to stay beside her. "Well," he said, thinking hard on her question, "if you take a deep breath, and you blow the air out, it only goes so far, and then it just…isn't there. It's gone."

She stopped then, and looked at him, and she said, "Oh, yeah," having a realization based on his example. "You're right." Then she began walking again, saying, "I'm Kathleen Dowdy. Pleased to meet you," but she was looking around in her restless way as she spoke.

"Hank Wenslow."

"Yeah, you told me."

"Didn't know if you heard."

"I did."

They took four more steps in silence, and then Hank said, "I don't recognize you—from around here," and then, without realizing it, he held his breath.

"A little over a month here so far," she said, and Hank let out the breath, nodding his head at the ground, where his eyes were cast, and then bringing them up to Kathleen Dowdy, or maybe to the goddess Chalchiuhtlicue, as they walked on.

"I'm helping out in the dry cleaners," she said. "I was on my way to Wisconsin, and my car was stolen with my purse in it. You didn't hear about that?" He shook his head as she gave him a quick toss of her dark eyes. "I'm making some money so I don't end up at my aunt's house without a penny. She doesn't like me anyway."

He nodded again, absorbing the information, and noticing that after Barbara's Beauty Parlor and the shop where the Dutchman painted signs and Joe Kosloski's gas station, just twenty steps ahead, they would be at the end of the town with only bare highway stretching the mile to the lumber yard and the gravel pit. His third fist was tightening, and his chest had frozen, too, so that he could feel his heartbeat. "Could it be?" his mind was asking, and then shouting, "What the hell *if*?"

"Where you going?" he asked her.

"Wisconsin."

"No, I mean…now."

She began cutting across the corner of an empty lot toward Hart's Road. "Where I stay. I got a room at the Rosteads'. You know the Rosteads?"

"Yeah." Then he had to think quickly, because she was marching through the weeds of the field at her businesslike pace. "Mind if I…walk along?"

She sent him two sudden and practiced looks, wary looks, one a quick brush of his face, the other a glance at his left hand where his dulled golden band was prominent.

"I just…I want to see how low the channel's got," he said, "with all this…lack of rain. You know, if you keep walking down Hart's Road, there's a channel to the lake."

She was staring ahead again, aiming herself at the gravel

road and the houses there. "Yeah, I go down there. It's peaceful. I change my clothes and go down there after work."

At the mention of her clothes, he glanced at her full skirt, remembering the rise of it with her legs revealed, and studying the color of the shiny fabric as it caught and released the sunlight, changing from light to dark green, but definitely green. And by glancing at her lower body, he brought his purpose to his mind. He couldn't help imagining the hair down there that would be as crow-black as the hair on her head, and he felt himself flushing as his heart increased with the memory of what he must do. His face felt feverish, and he must have made a sound in his throat because she flicked him another glance.

"You all right?"

"Yeah. Warm today."

"Well, I have to go fast," she said as her shoes met the gravel road, and they turned toward the houses. "Mrs. Rostead made a pound cake for me to take to work, and I forgot, so I'm getting it now, 'cause the owners, the Keaneses, are taking it over to the parents of that girl. Did you hear a girl died, crashed her car? She was eighteen."

"Yes. It's a shame."

"She came in to Keanes's once, for the cleaning. So weird to think she just popped out of the world now. Like she walked out a door or something. So, you live here?"

"Not in town," Wenslow said. "I'm a farmer."

"Uh-huh."

"All corn this year."

"Mm."

"Where were you coming from—in your car? When it was stolen."

"Chicago. I live in Chicago."

He was silent for five more steps, the Rostead house looming closer. He swallowed and asked, "Ever been to Mexico?"

"Nope. Well, here I am," and she made a quick turn to the flagstones of the walkway, moving toward the front door.

"Ever fish," he said hurriedly, "in that channel?"

"Haven't fished since I was a girl in Wisconsin. I liked it, but you don't fish in Chicago. I guess people fish in Lake Michigan, but not me. It's just too darn big. Bye."

She reached the steps to the porch and marched on, her dressy shoes loud on the old wood, and when she snatched the handle of the screen door, she had to pause and turn around because she knew he was still there, watching her, and she wanted to examine the expression on his face. It was worry and longing, she decided, and it was so powerful that she hesitated in the doorway.

Wenslow said the word without preparation. "Rain." She stared at him, and he made a valorous effort for more speech. "I'm trying to keep my corn alive, but it won't rain."

She nodded, drawn in by the ache she saw in his eyes. It didn't look to her like an aching for corn.

"Just…crazy for rain," he said, and that's all he had.

"Well, luck to you," she said, and went inside.

He half ran to his truck and sped to the bar near the train station, looking for news of Albingo and where the man might be staying. Ed Tramer was hefting boxes and cleaning beer taps, his bar not yet operational, and he told Wenslow that Albingo had gone east near McHenry where Highway 120 was under repair, hoping for a road job, and then he asked, "Why you looking for him?"

Wenslow's eyes dropped down to the old, scarred bar top and then looked through it, repeating the question to himself and answering, in his mind, "To see if it might be her, if she might be here after all, if it might be true because of the green skirt and black hair and her coming here at the time of the drought and even because of the wind that introduced her, baring her legs like a sign, an ancient Aztec sign," and what he wanted, what he saw in his mind was the face of Albingo as Wenslow told the man about Kathleen Dowdy and all the clues, and he created, on Albingo's face, a slowly growing smile and then a nod, a nod of certainty. But what Wenslow said to Ed Tramer was "…just… I have some work for him, after all. Fence posts." Tramer nodded and poured a free shot because the tall farmer looked so lost. Wenslow nodded a thanks and fingered the shot glass, searching the bronze-colored liquid to find his thoughts and found them seriously questioning his own sanity.

"You happen to know where he's stayin'?"

"No, Hank, no idea. He said he'd look around up there for a place. He's pretty sure of getting a job 'cause he can drive a dozer. Y'know, a guy can do all right for himself if he can drive a dozer."

Wenslow began a series of nods that went on and on without his knowing it, because he had created Albingo's face in his mind, and was busy watching that face as he told Albingo the news about Kathleen Dowdey and then sought the man's advice. Then he erased that moving picture and looked at Tramer.

"What d'you know about him—Albingo?"

Tramer shrugged. "Well, I know he's smart."

Wenslow began spreading a small, eager smile. "He is? He's smart?"

"Yep. You know Don Lopez, works in the bank in Liberty-ville?"

"Sure, sure, I know 'im. Why?"

"Well, him and Albingo were both in here last week, and they started talkin' in Spanish, and Don said the guy was smart, said he talked a pretty high Spanish."

"A high Spanish. That's good!"

Tramer was surprised at the strength of Wenslow's reaction. "Good? Well, anyway Don said the guy seemed like an educated man. Some kind of teacher, I guess."

"A teacher! That's great!"

The bartender narrowed his eyes at Wenslow. "Great? Uhh, yeah. I guess it's great. Why?"

"Well, Ed, it means he knows what he's talkin' about, right?"

"Uh-huh. I guess so. Means he's not just a workin' stiff if he can...y'know...like I said..." Tramer was trailing off, still mystified.

"If he can what?" Wenslow was pressing him.

"Well...drive a dozer." Tramer went back to his preparations for his bar while Wenslow stared into infinity, his hope rising, and that's when Tramer asked, "You hear about the Bridger girl?" He caught Wenslow's nod and added, "Don't seem fair when a kid is taken, does it?"

"Look who you're talking to!" Wenslow shouted inside his mind. "Yeah, it's awful for the Bridgers, but look who the hell you're talking to, Ed! Is he just plain forgotten — our little baby? It wasn't that long ago, and it was in the goddamn paper!" But the story had covered just three inches, a story as brief as the tiny child.

Wenslow remembered the young reporter who came to their door, all nerves and compassion. They knew him, the Cotterman kid. He had to ask. It was his job. "Just your thoughts," he had said, face flushed. Sandra even asked him if he wanted a glass of water, but when he said no thanks, that was all she had. She sat down in a kitchen chair, looking at nothing, and Wenslow had walked out the door, leaving the reporter quoteless. The paper had reported that the Wenslows were "silent in their grief," and that was all, and then the town, Wenslow realized now, had simply forgotten.

Tramer sighed loudly then and blew away Wenslow's memories with another change of subject. "Sure is something. Man oh man, never *ever* seen a summer…*you* ever seen a summer this dry?"

Wenslow felt his fingers tighten on the tiny glass and felt his other fist clench on the bar top and his third fist grab him in the middle. He stiffened from the pain and suddenly lifted the whiskey and drank it all down, making a face, and when his face untwisted, he put the empty glass down with a sharp knock and said, with sudden certainty, "It's a curse," looking Ed Tramer in the eyes.

"Guess so," Ed said, thrown again by Wenslow's shifting moods. "But…y'know…" And he shrugged with his shoulders high and his empty palms upward. "What the hell can you do?"

Wenslow answered with powerful conviction, saying, "We'll see!" And then he walked out the door.

He drove to the hardware in Round Lake, one town away, where few people were likely to know him, and he bought a spin-casting rod and reel and two shiny lures, low priced, but not the cheapest. The man at the counter asked, "What're you fishin' for?"

Wenslow said it again, "We'll see!"

When he put the rod in the back of his truck, he looked across the street at Lassiter's Clothing Store and was struck by an idea that nearly defeated him, but he pushed through the discomfort, knowing his corn could not take another dry week and have any hope of survival.

He angled across the street, hoping to move into and out of the store without seeing anyone who knew him, but there she was, the woman he had remembered earlier today, Myrna Gresha, and he pretended he hadn't seen her, even as she stared at him in passing. He kept his eyes away from hers because people said she could read your mind. People said many things about Myrna, a dowser of water and finder of lost things, and he didn't believe it all, but he kept his eyes from her so she could not see his betrayal of his wife and his secret mission to Lassiter's.

He walked into the store and sucked in a long breath and searched for a gift for Kathleen Dowdy. He was in unfamiliar country, and the attention of the two saleswomen only increased his agitation. He was buying a present, is all he told them, and then ignored their stream of suggestions and moved toward a print blouse of many colors, but it was mostly green, and he knew it would go with her skirt, and it looked joyful, as a gift should look, and it might make Kathleen Dowdy smile at him, and Chali-something take this as an offering and grant him the opportunity to do…what he had to do. There wasn't much time because the moon would begin to wane tonight, and so he bought the blouse, a medium, he decided, and had the women fold it and box it and put a ribbon on the box. He hid the box under the seat of the truck and drove home to start work on the fence posts and count the hours until Kathleen was free of work and possibly going down to the channel for the peace she received from the reeds and the willow trees and the quiet brown water.

He drove to his farm and stopped at the house, where he drank from the faucet of the kitchen sink and avoided the eyes of his wife, feeling a powerful throb of guilt along with his headache because of his plan with Kathleen and the fishing rod that rattled in his truck bed and the blouse hidden in the cab. If he had met Sandy's eyes, he might have seen an extra measure of softness there for him, because she had spent hours thinking about last night and his tenderness and the kiss and the tears upon her bare belly, and her love for him had come closer to the surface than she usually allowed.

She waited for his eyes because she wanted to send this message to him, like a dose of medicine for his aching over the corn and his terrible desperation that was familiar to her from before, from the before they never mentioned. She couldn't say it, because the words would be too much. Flying out of her, they might alert whatever it was that punished her for any feeling that was too big, any loving that was too bare. She imagined a hawk circling in the sky, waiting for her to throw her arms around her hurting husband or laugh too hard or sing or even think of having another child, and this hawk would come down, and in one fierce swoop, take something else away.

Wenslow didn't give her his eyes, but busied himself making and wrapping a sandwich for his lunch. She offered to make him a thermos of coffee, and he thanked her, but didn't turn to her. She made the coffee and warmed the milk as he liked it and mixed them together and poured this into the thermos, and she had the thought that with the strawberries she had she could make them a shortcake for supper, but then she erased the thought because a shortcake would be too much, because they both loved shortcake, and the pleasure it would bring might be too much pleasure for the hawk to allow, as if pleasure was pride, and a sin, and all of this because a child had been given and taken away, and some parts of Sandra were torn in the taking and never healed.

Wenslow drove out to the far northern border of their hundred acres to replace the rotted posts and restring the wire, and Sandra watered her garden from the hose and pulled weeds and watched a flock of blackbirds burst across the windy sky like a load of buckshot and then weave and turn all as one, dancing on the wing. The sight thrilled her, and the wind cooled the day and seemed to sharpen the sunlight, and she simply had to move, to claim her partnership in the natural world by walking in it and taking notice. She went through the farmyard and the one fallow field, took off her shoes and raised her dress to wade across the almost dry creek and walked on to a low hill where an old bent oak was surviving one more summer.

She had visited this hilltop and this tree in all seasons and all moods and even brought her child here in that brief visit that was his life. She had wanted to bury his tiny body in this spot when he was taken, but she never spoke that thought, moving gutted through her grief, following the expected path of funeral, cemetery, and gravestone, hardly speaking. But she felt that the soul of Bryan had somehow found its way here and rested beneath the oak that dipped its twisted branches all the way to the ground, as if it bent to hold him, and she had, last year, buried the purple martin here that had been killed by the neighbor boys, and she would visit its grave, which she had marked with a frame of stones.

She bent forward on the steepest slope, gaining the top with her heart drumming and a light skin of sweat on her body, and then she stopped, staring down at the too-dry grass where her eye was caught by the most vivid scarlet on a field of the deepest black. It was the body of a red-winged blackbird, and she looked bewildered, and then she looked above, searching for the likely killer, the hawk, but the sky was empty of birds now, and she looked again at the fallen red-wing, its neck twisted all around and its wings in death's disorder, and then her eyes trailed to the trunk of the oak and to the nestling place between two raised roots where she had buried the martin. She walked more closely to the tree and saw that the martin's grave was as she left it, only more hidden by the grasses, and then she walked back to the red-wing and this time knelt beside it. She touched the softness of its feathers near its proud, flamboyant splash of red. She eased its wings into line, and then she lifted the bird in her cupped hands and sat back to make a lap. She laid the bird there, which, without life, weighed hardly more than a shadow on her skirt.

She remained that way for a long time, leaning back on her hands, looking from bird to tree to sky while a thought seeped inside of her, more than a thought, a revelation. If her child had died because she wanted him too much, and if the purple martin had died because she began to care too much for the nesting birds in the barn, then why did the red-wing die? She had never seen the red-wing, and her love had never touched it.

The seeping in of the revelation took about half an hour, while the breeze blew through her hair and over the grasses and the oak leaves and the feathers in her lap, and another half hour for this revelation to harden into words, three words, and she said these words in her mind like prayers to the old tree, to the grave, to the spirit of her lost boy, to the remains that rested on her skirt, and then she said the words aloud, very softly. She said, "Death comes anyway."

Wenslow had set three of the fence posts and then eaten his

lunch while he walked his corn rows again and inspected the dryness and touched the stalks and leaves and sent a promise through his hands that he would not let death come, that he would, in fact, bring rain, and he imagined himself as a dry stalk lined up with all the others, patient, but drooping, dying of thirst, and then he imagined the rain coming, pattering on his own leaves and running down the stalk of him and soaking the ground where he stood to reach his roots and save him, and he felt the moisture rise in his human breast and throat as he pictured this, pictured each of the thousands of stalks drinking and thriving and growing like healthy children.

He didn't finish the final post, worried that he might not be ready in time to find Kathleen at the channel. He drove to the farmhouse, but Sandy wasn't there, and he was glad because she would have asked where he was going, and he would have had to lie. He washed and put on a fresh shirt, combed his hair and then smiled into the mirror, but the smile was forced, and he let it fall away, and then he saw the doubt. He saw the futility in his eyes and in the part in his hair and the extra-close shave, and he didn't want to look at this, at the possibility that all of it was pathetic, so he turned away and buttoned his shirt and slapped the dust from his jeans, not aware that Sandy was returning from the hilltop and glad to see his truck parked at the house.

She decided she wouldn't say anything about the dead red-wing, because they didn't speak of things dying, but she wanted to be close to him while she thought it over. If death comes any-way, then why fear the hawk, and why whisper and not shout, and why not laugh? The questions swelled like balloons inside of her and frightened her and excited her, too, so to calm herself she put her vision on the old truck, and stared at it a moment and decided she better clean out the leavings of his lunch and the thermos that might still be in the cab. She opened the passenger door and stepped up into the truck to reach the thermos, and the heel of her shoe crushed something, and when she looked down, she saw the corner of a white box showing from under the seat. She pulled it out. It was gift-wrapped with a red bow and had the name LASSITER'S CLOTHING STORE on it, and she stared at this with wonder.

It was months until her birthday and even longer until their next anniversary, and then she thought of last night and the tenderness he had brought to the bed. He had reached for her last night, and was reaching for her again now, with this gift, and change was coming at her, from her loving husband and from the red-wing, too, and she wanted to meet it and embrace it if she could. She prayed that she could as she replaced the box under the seat and went into the kitchen with the wax paper and the thermos, and she washed out the thermos and wondered what she might say to her husband.

Wenslow heard his wife at the kitchen sink and this nearly panicked him. He didn't want to see her now, so he left the bathroom and walked quietly to the front of the house, out the door and then quickly around to his truck. He entered the cab and started the engine and drove away without glancing at the house or listening in case she might call after him. It would have cracked his heart to hear her call after him.

Sandra heard the truck start and stopped her washing, but by the time she went to the window, she saw only the dust of his leaving and wondered if he was going back into the corn, and she began to plan for his return and what she would say, what she might give him in trade for his surprise for her from Lassiter's.

—.—

WENSLOW drove to the town, now worrying that he might be too early. He passed the dry cleaners shop twice, glancing in and seeing Mrs. Keanes behind the counter and no one else in sight. He drove to Hart's Road and turned toward the channel, passing the Rosteads' home, where there were no signs of life, and driving on to where the road ended, he moved the truck into the weeds near the walking path to the water. He pulled the fishing rod and lures from his truck and made sure to peel the price tag off the handle and then he walked down to the grassy banks where cattails were dying and the willows were hanging low, their branches mirrored in the water that seemed stagnant but moved slowly at its bottom to join with Indian Lake a mile and a half away.

He stopped to tie on a small shining lure, and his hands reminded him how nervous he was. He scouted the curving banks as far as he could see and stopped to listen and found himself alone. He cast into the water and reeled in slowly, not expecting or even wanting a strike. He only wanted to be in the act of fishing when she came. He moved on along the meandering channel, casting now and then, and in a while he heard voices and came upon two boys fishing with long bamboo poles and bright red-and-white bobbers floating out in front of them as they lazed on the bank. They sat up at the sight of an adult and became quiet and shy, and they caused Wenslow to draw more inside himself, feeling a sweat break on his skin because he knew them. One was Buddy Bensen, a neighbor boy whom Sandra had hired to kill the starlings in their barn, and the other was Freddy Carli, who worked for his father at the Tip Top Grocery where he and Sandra kept a credit account, and so in Wenslow's mind these boys stood for his neighbors and for the town, and so, through them, the people of Indian Lake were watching him now, and he tried to be at ease and made poor work of it.

"They bitin'?" he asked them.

Freddy said, "Not yet."

Then Wenslow asked about the bait they were using because it seemed a normal question to ask, and Buddy said, "I'm usin' a nightcrawler, and he's usin' bread," because in those days the children along the channel caught bullheads and some-times even carp with mashed and rolled-up pieces of Wonder Bread. Few people ate those bottom-feeding fish, but they were the largest in the channel and put up the best fight, and that's what they wanted, these boys, to feel the desperate struggle that bent their poles almost double and pulled at their hands and arms. They wanted to experience the fight for life over death, because what's more intense or has higher stakes than that, whether it concerns a fish or a stalk of corn or a human child?

In a moment, after he had cast again and was reeling in, he asked them, casually, "Seen anybody else down here?" and saw the boys glance at each other.

Freddy said, "That woman. There's a woman down that way," and he pointed Wenslow farther down the curving banks out of sight, and Wenslow nodded and pretended to be engrossed in his fishing, but, side-step by side-step, moving along the way the boy had pointed, and, when he was gone, Freddy looked at his friend, and their small smiles were half humor and half excitement because they had noticed that Wenslow had cast and reeled in too quickly and wasn't truly fishing, and because everybody knew the man was acting very strange that summer and because he was now moving toward that new woman, that pretty woman who worked at Keanes's cleaners, and they wondered what was going to happen.

Wenslow heard something splash in the water, and when he turned the next curve of bank, there was Kathleen Dowdy, sitting on the ground, hugging her knees. She wore blue jeans with the cuffs rolled and tennis shoes and a white shirt, her hair gathered behind in a rubber band, and she looked to him like a picture in a magazine. She had a pile of several stones nearby, and she reached for another one to throw when she saw him and froze the action.

"Oh, hi," he said, with what he hoped looked like a surprised grin.

She didn't smile, but nodded once, and he thought he saw some interest in her eyes. Then she threw the stone and they both watched the splash and the ripples.

"I like to do that once in a while," she said, "when it gets too quiet."

He came to stand beside her, and he cast his line, but too far, and struck the opposite bank. It didn't catch, though, so he was able to jerk the lure into the water and reel it in slowly, recovering something of his self-possession.

"I guess I scared 'em all away with the stones."

"That's okay," he said, sitting beside her, but looking out at the water. "Channel's pretty low." He nodded toward the water as if she didn't know where it was. "Lake's low, too. No damn rain...for too damn long."

"So, farmers really talk like that—about the weather?"

He looked at her then, and saw her first smile for him, a small, wry one that she aimed at the channel. He tried to smooth his voice and get the nerves out of it and to ignore the hand clenching at his intestines. "I guess I can talk about other things."

"Like what?" She threw another stone. They watched the rings widen into a watery target with the splash as its bull's eye.

"You got any Mexican blood?"

"What?" She allowed a major smile then, and stretched out in the grass and leaned back on her elbows. "Irish through and through."

He reddened and braved a glance at her lying beside him, her face made beautiful by the smile, her shoulders back and breasts pushed against her shirt, and reality struck him like a hammer and reminded him of his intent, that he was here to convince this stranger, this Irish woman from Chicago, to make love with him, and then to make sure that, within this act, she came to orgasm, and this had to happen before the further waning of the moon, and he reeled from this hammer blow and felt crazed and defeated.

Then the other part of his mind spoke, the smaller part that was stubbornly defending his probable insanity by saying that if this was Chali-something in disguise, wouldn't she allow this to happen? It was why she was here. It was part of the plan. Wouldn't she be willing to do her part? And think of the corn, this part of his mind said, playing its ace. Think of your promise to the withering corn. He thought his inner fist was as tight as fists could be, but it tightened even more, and he put a hand there, and she asked him, "You sick?"

"No. So…you're sure you never been to Mexico?"

"No, you?"

"No," Wenslow said, and then said nothing more.

"So, why'd you ask me?"

He shook his head slowly, eyes studying the brown water.

"Here," she said, and he saw that she was sitting up and handing him one of her stones. "Throw it in."

He did.

"See?" she said. "You're a lot better at doing things than you are at talking. Now kiss me."

Wenslow turned to her so suddenly, he nearly wrenched his neck. Her smile was wry again and knowing, and she raised one eyebrow, and the eyebrow asked, "Well?" He didn't move, and she chuckled at his surprise and immobility. "I don't think you're here to fish for fish," she said. "And I want to be able to say that I kissed a farmer in Indian Lake. I just want to be able to say that. So?"

He looked afraid and awed by this opportunity and much more serious than lustful, but he slid closer to her, and, all in one motion, put a hand behind her head and bent close to put his lips on her smile, and it was a soft kiss and then hard and pressing with some passion in it, and it was the only serious kiss he had ever made with anyone else since his first date with Sandra.

When he pulled back, he saw that her smile was still on her mouth and also in her dark eyes where there was mischief and pleasure, too, as if she were appraising him. "Nice," she said. "Now I can say it—that I did it." She stood up and brushed at the back of her jeans. "And you can say you kissed that Chicago woman who was working at the dry cleaners. 'Cause a couple have tried, you know. But you're the one."

He rose, too, standing tilted and unsure on the bank. "I'm the one," he said, giving the words a possible mythological meaning.

"Yep. And I'm the fish that got away."

Alarm thumped in his chest. "Where? Where you going?"

"The police found my car in Waukegan. I'll get it tomorrow."

"And…go?"

She sighed and looked at the water again, hands on her hips. "Don't know if I want to go on to Wisconsin or just give it up and get back to Chicago. I'm not as mad at my boyfriend anymore, and I've had enough country to last me about a hundred years. You know, I'll take noise if noise is what it takes.

Give me noise, and something to actually *do* at night. So, I guess I won't see you." She sent a hand out to him for a shake, like a man.

Both his hands came up slowly, and for all their size and roughness, they wrapped hers gently and held it softly. "Wait," he said, and the word came out small and dry and cracked.

"Wait for what?" She didn't try to take her hand away.

"Tonight," he said, and he had no other words prepared, but an idea was forming, desperate and sudden, as his third fist twisted inside so that he nearly cried out.

"Tonight? What's to do at night around here?"

"Ever…ever come down here at night, to the channel?"

"What do you have in mind, some night fishing?" She hung her wry smile out there for him to see, and he tried to match it, but he couldn't move his mouth and there was no smile in him.

"Yeah," he said, and the word thudded like a stone.

"Too many bugs." And she pulled a bit at her hand, but he couldn't let her go. There was a very quiet life-and-death struggle happening there, with thousands of drying corn stalks at stake and the pain in a man's middle that had turned to fire.

"There's a way," he said, remembering what he and Sandra had called "picnics" in the days before the child. These were wanderings into a fallow field with a blanket and a bit of food, but truthfully, they were moving out into the tall wind-combed grasses to lie with each other and make love, so that the word, "picnic" came to mean their sexual pleasure, even in their bed, as in, "Sleepy?" "Mm, a little. You?" "No. Let's have a picnic," and then the laughter in the dark and the beginning of their tangling.

"What way?" Kathleen Dowdy asked, not fighting for her hand and leaving her smile in place.

"You…take a blanket, and you spray it—with insect repellant, spray all the bottom, and then when you lay it out, they stay away—most of 'em."

"I thought farmers weren't supposed to be smart."

He worked very hard to construct a grin and failed, leaving the ruin there. "You have to be," he said. "For the crops. Have to be. So…it'll be…good here tonight."

"It will?"

"I mean…yeah, the moon. The moon'll be…in the water, almost a full moon. Almost. So… Will you come?"

"Look at you," she said, her smile growing. "Big tall farmer, and you look like a little boy. Now let me go."

His hands let go of her, but not his eyes, not his question, more prayer than question. "You'll come? Kathleen?"

"Maybe." She started to go, her smile sent back to him. "And my friends don't call me Kathleen."

"Kathy? You'll come? When the moon rises?"

"They call me 'Charlie'," she said. "And maybe."

"Charlie." He said the word with what sounded like a last breath, his mouth unhinging and his hand moving to the pain in his center. His tone made her pause, and as they stared, fifteen feet apart, he said, "Chali-something," and it's not certain she heard him. She made no answer, but walked backwards a few steps on the path before she turned, leaving her smile framed in the humid afternoon air.

She would come. She had to come because she was Chali-something, and she had kissed him, and the plan was unfolding, and he stood there a moment, tilting on the channel bank and had to swallow and swallow and try to steady his breath. His inner fist was throbbing, and he was sending a rush of apologies to Sandy from his mind, saying that he was sorry he was seeing another woman and that he would be having sex with this woman tonight, and he was also sorry that he had told this woman about the blanket and the repellant because that was their secret that had to do with their picnics, and their picnics were their intimacy, and he was so, so sorry to be dishonoring their intimacy, but it was all for the corn, for the stalks of corn that were in his care, because he couldn't let another life pass through his hands and fall away. He could not.

He walked back to his truck and looked at the fishing rod in his hand as if it was some alien object he had never seen before. He put it in the truck bed and entered the cab and remembered the blouse that was gift-wrapped on the floor under the seat. That would be for tonight, the offering to Chali. She would unwrap it in the moonlight and thank him and that would be the oil that would smooth their way to the blanket, and once on the blanket there would be the clothing to remove and once they were naked there would be... He had to be able to do this. He had to move through the mystery to find the hidden place and release the magic that would save the life of four thousand stalks of corn and unclench the killing fist in the center of himself.

Sandra felt herself quicken when she heard his truck, and a smile came to her, and her automatic reaction was to rein back the quickening and erase the smile, but then she let them go ahead, at least halfway. This burgeoning courage of hers was like a set of new clothes that needed breaking in and getting used to. She was disappointed when she saw out the window that he wasn't coming in but walking away into the corn. She hurried out to the porch and called, "Supper's almost ready!"

He shouted back without turning, "Okay. I'll be there."

She watched him, wishing she could keep him out of the cornfield. She had words now that would help him, that would let him know what she knew, what she had learned from the red-wing, and how she felt, how she was beginning to feel. She watched him disappear into the corn and sighed and returned to her stove.

— · —

WENSLOW touched one stalk of corn, letting it stand for them all and felt its dryness and its fragile hold on the earth and said out loud to the plant, "Tonight," and the word was an oath. When the moon was high, all this would end, all this waiting and worry and pain, and he almost believed it completely. He had locked his doubt into one small damp room of his mind, and he didn't want to listen to it pounding on the door and shouting warnings. He walked back to the house, thinking of what he'd say to Sandy in order to get away after supper, and he checked the horizon to judge how much of the used-up faded daylight was left. An hour and a half before moonrise.

As Wenslow ate his supper, he found that he couldn't swallow very well. The fist in his belly had grown claws, and he thought he might be bleeding inside. Sandra saw his distraction and his worry, and she ached for him and thought she should send him the first of her messages. She had created them over the last few hours and wrapped them like gifts, and she unwrapped the first one and said, tentatively, "There's a Martin and Lewis film tonight."

He looked at her as if he hadn't understood the words or assembled them in the right order. "At the drive-in," she added, and he saw the small smile that was beginning to glow softly in her eyes like a nightlight, but then it trembled away. They hadn't been to the drive-in since before the birth and death of Bryan, and a Martin and Lewis film would be a brave choice because it would make them laugh out loud.

"Oh…well…" He tried to swallow. "Don't know, I…" He put his eyes back on his plate and made a weak shrug.

She looked at his plate, too, and saw the food hardly disturbed, and this worried her. She searched her mind for talk, not wanting to rush into the next message she was holding for him, not yet.

He was searching, too, because of the smothering silence, and he scrambled through his memory of the day, a day full of secrets, for something that was safe to say. He thought of the teenager, the auto crash and the dead Bridger girl, and wondered if anyone had called Sandra and told her, but no, because the news of a death, a child's death would have shaken her, and there would be no smile in her eyes. He was about to give her this news now because he could think of nothing else, but he fought against the words, fought and won, not only to protect his wife from a tale of death, but for the girl herself, for Emily Bridger. He didn't want to use her this way, to toss her on the table like a poker chip. He was ashamed of so much that he had done this day and ashamed of what he planned for tonight, and he wouldn't add another shame, so he released the girl, and released the anger he had felt when people told him the news of her death, forgetting that he and Sandy had also suffered this most heart-tearing of losses. He wouldn't hold on to that bitterness either, and so he sighed and let go of Emily Bridger with a sad salute.

Sandra also had nothing that would penetrate the silence except those words that pressed her for release, those fresh-minted words she'd been saving for hours and practicing, and she gave way and said, "Hen, I made strawberry shortcake." She even lifted her chin a bit when she said it, daring the hawk, and keeping her chin high even as it shook.

This brought his stare to her again, seeing the light increase in her eyes, and the sight was a kind of miracle. Strawberry shortcake and a drive-in movie—it was as if she were offering him their old life, their life before, and he couldn't understand it. What had happened? Why was she smiling that way, that little grin as she ate her food, her eyes on her plate, as if the pork chop was amusing and the peas and the potatoes somehow funny, and he couldn't keep from looking at her, while his clawed fist tightened and bled and his mind shouted, "Honey, honey, I have to tear away from you tonight. I have to tear myself away. It's my only chance."

"I know," she said, as if she had heard his mind, and his thoughts screeched to a full stop and his eyes did not blink as she raised her smile from her food and shined it at him, full force. "I saw the box in your truck, and I know you got me something."

He remained immobile. He could not make a smile, and he could not tell her a lie and he could not tell her the truth. He wished he could sit there for a year and look at her, at her shining face. He slowly put his hands on the table, steadied himself and prayed that the fist in his gut would not kill him when he pushed upward. He rose from the table and walked to the door and out of the house to his truck, pulling open the door and reaching in, bringing out the box and walking back to his kitchen and all of this while hardly breathing. She had given him that smile, that old smile, and he had to give her something in return, and it would be this blouse, and then he would go, and he would have to do his work tonight without the offering of a gift, because he couldn't take from his wife what had pleased her so and brought back her blinding smile.

He placed the box in her lap and she touched it, looking as if she might break out and laugh with pleasure at the very idea of a gift. "Thank you. Thank you, Hen."

He swallowed and said quickly, "It's a blouse, and…they didn't have your size, so it'll be a little big."

She nodded with her smile in place and worked carefully at the knot of the bow in order to save the ribbon. When it was off, she began to open the box, and then looked at him, and she was suddenly the girl he had first met, excited and animated, saying, "I'll put it on now!" and rising quickly and almost running to the bedroom.

He watched her leave with all the waters of his body rising to his throat and causing his third fist to clench and twist so that he doubled over as soon as she was out of sight. After two labored breaths, he went into the mudroom and opened a cupboard and took from there the picnic blanket, unused for two years, and he placed it just outside the back door so he could grab it on the way to his truck. Then he hurried back inside and searched for and found the insect repellant and went out again and tossed the can on top of the blanket. Before he closed the back door, he heard the wind rising and moving through his corn, rustling the dying leaves, and he imagined those leaves waving, waving like arms, tiny arms, child-size arms, waving at him.

He stood in the hall and stared at the open bedroom door. He could hear the soft rustle of clothing in there. He took several breaths for calmness and the management of pain, and he thought of what he'd say. "Sorry. Sorry, honey, but I have to go for a while, just for a while, to talk to some of the men about the corn, to talk about the rain and the corn." That's what he would say, and he practiced.

—·—

ONLY the lamp on her dresser was lit, and Sandra didn't pause to turn on the overhead, but quickly put the box down in the lamplight and pulled at the lid. What she saw, when she spread open the tissue paper, was the finest gift she had ever received because it told her how much her husband loved her and how well he knew her wounded heart. She picked up the blouse with a soft outcry and put it to her face like a towel and wept into it before she could pull it away and study it again. She was wearing a dress, and this she unzipped and let fall and kicked away as she pulled the blouse over her bra and half-slip and stood before the mirror. She stood a long while, and then called out, softly, "Hen?"

Wenslow stepped into the low light of the bedroom and came to her, and as he reached her she turned and embraced him, her wet face pressed to his shirt, and when she could speak, she said, "You brought me all my birds," and she sobbed once against him, but the sob was half laughter, and Wenslow was all confusion until he looked past her sandy hair to the shoulder of her blouse where he saw that the print, the small designs he had not paid attention to in the store, were tiny birds, many different birds, a hummingbird, a robin, a purple martin... And she drew back her face then, her smile part liquid but bright in the lamplight, and his love for her shook him, and he had to kiss her. He would kiss her, he thought, and when they were through, he would have to tell her his lie and he would have to go, but he would kiss her, and he did, and they made one mouth out of two starving mouths, and in their kissing their bodies tightened, and Wenslow's right hand slid down past the blouse over the silky curve of her buttocks to the lace at the hem of her short half-slip and gripped her thigh, and with his other hand at the small of her back, he lifted her against him, so that her feet dangled and one shoe slipped off, and he held her there as they breathed and then joined their mouths again.

He pulled against her thigh, and her knee lifted to his hip as she hung suspended against him, and then she lifted her other knee, wrapping him with her legs, and he felt himself become hard, and he thought, god...do you think she would? Do you think I could? Could I do this, and then leave her when the moon rises? Could I do that? But while his mind was deciding, his body was moving in slow, awkward steps toward the bed, two bodies wrapped into one, moving through the near darkness of the bedroom, and he wondered if she would whisper "no" between their kissing and make him stop, but she didn't, and so he reached the bed and used all his strength to lay her down gently and lay himself beside her and half on top of her, their mouths locking again, and his hands moving on her and brushing away her clothes.

When he had bared her, he felt her breath shudder, and he paused and whispered, "Sandy?" She didn't speak, and her broken breath continued, and he whispered, "You afraid?"

He pulled back enough to see her face in the low light, and she nodded that she was afraid, but she said, within the shuddering, "It's okay," and her eyes were staring hard and deep, and he saw everything there, the fear and the wanting, and the loss, too, and the breaking and the tiny boy and the corn, and then she was helping him shed his clothes, and he was moving her legs apart, deciding he would give her all that he could, everything, and he entered her, and she stiffened, but did not stop kissing him and so he went on, moving within her slowly, with care and with joy and then abandon, and he felt a shock move through her, and she spasmed and whimpered and then cried out, nearly a scream of release, and her breath was gone, and she couldn't catch it, but the moaning that came with tears and with the gasping for air had the sound of pleasure in it, and her smile came, mouth open, with a sobbing that was both a reclaiming of something and a letting go, and Wenslow felt a great, mountainous awe as he watched her and felt her in his arms, and he realized that the power and the joy that filled him came from her and from inside himself, where his third fist began to open, and when a fist lets go of itself, it disappears, and he was free of it.

While she sobbed with erratic breath, Wenslow felt tears of his own, and he knew that he would not leave his wife tonight, because his dry cracked self was alive again, they were both alive again, and the dying corn and the dead little boy were not the end of them, and so when the moon rose nearly full, it struck the window and lit the bed and settled in to watch the long, unfolding picnic there.

Kathleen Dowdy never came to the channel that night. Her car was delivered at seven P.M. by a local policeman who hoped to impress her with the delivery and possibly get a date, but she declined, saying she was already packed and would leave that very night, and she added a sentence he didn't quite understand. She said, "I'm finished here anyway."

Laketown Dead

JUST ABOUT THREE AND A HALF MILES from the unpaved turn-off into the Wenslow farm, there is a stretch of the two-lane highway where the trees line both sides of the road, as if they'd come to watch the traffic or to stare at something, and it is on this particular day in July of '54 when Emily Bridger, a girl of eighteen, came into herself in a patch of these woods and saw those trees lit by the burning sun and by their own ancient chemistry. She came into herself slowly, first by recognizing that she had sight, because the leaves, in a hundred different renderings of green, could not be ignored, and then by feeling her chest fill and rise in a silent gasp of appreciation at the colors of the wildflowers chosen for this eternal summer ritual, and then she swallowed and licked her lips, and each sight and gesture was somehow very important. She didn't know why. She saw that she was standing. She held nothing in her hands.

She rubbed them together and left them clasped, just for the familiar feel of herself, and then she saw the boy.

He was ten or eleven, thin and pale and wearing a white t-shirt and red bathing trunks, the shortest crew-cut leaving him almost hairless and making his eyes appear even larger as he stared at her from twenty feet away, partly hidden by the trees, and then he was gone. She took a step and then another, but she couldn't see him, and she used her voice to shout, "Wait," but the word came out soft and broken and fell at her feet. She looked at her shoes standing on the dirt and vegetation, her usual scuffed pumps, and at her familiar skirt and blouse and then at the woods again, noticing a thick, scarred birch, its trunk savaged by recent wounds. She heard a humming and turned and saw the highway behind her and a passing car that had nothing to do with her. That's what she felt—that the car and its driver were separated from her by something vague and vast, and the feeling frightened her, the feeling of separation, so she looked for the boy again and began walking.

She moved through the woods easily. Her ankles and shins were bare, but she felt nothing touch her skin. She looked for the boy as she walked and never stumbled, and she found him crouched and watching her from behind a fallen trunk. He stood up slowly.

"People come for a few minutes, and then they're gone sometimes," he said.

Emily only looked at him.

"You're stayin', I guess." He sounded half tough and half afraid. He had no smile about him, but a tension in his face, his eyes narrowing on her and searching. "You know where you are?"

Emily shrugged, taking note of the rise and fall of her muscles and bones. "By the highway."

"Yeah, by the highway. So…are you stayin'?"

She looked away from the boy, through the trees toward the road, and she shrugged again for the feel of it, and she said, "Maybe I'll go home."

"You can't. You think you can but you can't."

"Why not?"

"Shit, I don't know. You think I know? I'm Billy Nester, who the hell are you?"

"Emily Brid…" She didn't say her whole name, because the vagueness in her mind was being overtaken by a certainty. It was happening slowly. "You died," she said. "Billy Nester drowned. A long time ago."

"Five goddamn years."

They stared at each other, the tough boy who was afraid she would leave, and the quiet girl feeling the certainty fill her like blood, instead of blood. She had the sense of dreaming while awake, everything cushioned, softened, not peaceful though, not completely peaceful. There was tension. There were questions.

"What happens now?" she asked him.

"Not a goddamn thing."

"You swear a lot for your age."

"I'd be sixteen now," he said.

Emily said, "Oh," but she said it to herself, taking in the

information, and in a minute she added, "We don't get older then."

"Hell no. What do I look like?" He was serious about the question, waiting for an answer. "I still look eleven, right?"

"Don't you ever look?" she wondered. "You could see your-self—in water."

"I don't go near water."

She nodded, understanding, and then asked, "What do I look like?"

"Sorta pretty."

"My hair…"

"It's okay. Combed, I guess."

She began to nod, and by the time she finished the gesture, she was back beside the highway, near the torn birch tree, and she didn't remember moving. The boy was beside her, pointing at the tree, asking her, "What about that?"

She remembered now, and the memory pushed her away. She chose a new direction and walked deeper into the forest. She didn't hear her own footsteps, but she felt them, or she felt the memory of footsteps. She caught her breath, or the memory of her breath, when she saw the old man. His face was fierce, his white hair rising from his blotched head like wild thoughts. She didn't turn away, but she was back at the birch tree again, and Billy Nester was beside her. She was sitting now, and staring at the cracks and gashes in the tree, and after a while, she said, "I just saw an old man."

"That's Fegg," Billy said. "Bastard."

And after another moment, she said, "I crashed into this tree. In my parents' car."

"Alone?" Billy asked.

She nodded and then she rose and said, "I'd better go home, just to…just to…"

Billy shrugged, still looking at the tree, and said, "Try it."

Then she was walking on Channel Drive, but not hearing the gravel under her shoes. She was looking ahead to her house, six houses on the right, and already seeing the roof, when she heard a car coming up behind her, and became afraid. She felt herself tighten, every part of her, as the car came on without slowing. She didn't close her eyes or even blink, but she was now standing in her front yard, and the car must have long passed because there was no sound and no dust in the air from the gravel.

Her yard looked as it always had, with twin oak trees that kept the sun from the house except in winter. There were a few leaves dotting the grass like torn paper, and the house was the same except for a black wreath on the door. There was no car in the driveway, and she wondered vaguely how her mother was getting to work because the car must be wrecked, and then she heard, through the windows and walls, the sound of the television, not even human, not a voice, but a tangle of music and shouting and noise, electric noise, and she pictured her father in his chair, watching, and the sickness, the old sickness made a grab for her, and she was suddenly half a mile away, running through the knee-high reeds near the channel, smelling the mud of the banks and thrusting out her hands because the wild berry bushes were in front of her, and she closed her eyes and waited for the thorns to slash her hands and catch her clothing as she forced her way through, but nothing touched her, and she opened her eyes and saw the brown channel water snaking slowly toward the lake, and on the water was the rippled reflection of herself, and the memory of the sickness caught her then and made her cry, and when no tears came, she opened her mouth and moaned because the memories were in her like thorns, and her moan became a wild cry of pain and shame and anger, too.

"What? What! What're you yellin' about?"

The cry collapsed in her throat as she saw the old man across the narrow channel, his white hair wild and his eyes fierce. He was barefoot and wore flannel pajamas, faded and fraying, and his jaw trembled as he shouted at her.

"You. You! What's all the yellin'? What've you got to yell about?"

"I...hit a tree." Emily spoke with her throat full.

"What?"

"I hit a tree...with my car. I died!"

"Died, hell. Died? So, you died. Keep your mouth shut about it. I was killed. Killed! And you come here cryin' and shoutin' like a goddamn girl."

"I *am* a girl!"

He took a step toward her, coming to the edge of his bank, his eyes at full power now, as if he had thrown a switch, and the power—of hate and wild anger—made her step back. "You ain't a girl! You're a dead girl! So what? I was killed. You ain't been killed with a goddamn pillow pressed down that takes all your air, takes your air and makes the daylight go and your arms are so weak, so weak and skinny, and I used to be strong! You were never strong. What did you have to give up, how many little years did you have? I had to give up seventy-one into that goddamn pillow, screamin', seventy-one years into that pillow that she pushed on me, and I couldn't stop her, and I felled trees! And I hefted logs and milled lumber and made a house from four trees and made a mill, and what did you ever do? What did you ever do?"

Emily was shaking, and knew that she should be feeling tears on her face, but she couldn't, and she couldn't taste them, and she wept without them and shouted back, "Nothing!"

"That's right. That's right! You never did nothing!"

"Nothing!" She was sobbing, and her words were broken roughly with sharp edges that hurt her chest and her throat. "I didn't do anything! I didn't say anything! I never said anything! I just let him do it!" She wanted to fall into the slow brown water, but when she moved, she was back at the birch tree where she had died, and she sank slowly and was sitting on the ground, her knees up and her face pressed against the bones of her knees. She knew Billy Nester was there, sitting beside her, and after a long while she raised her head, and she swallowed, though there were no tears to swallow, and she and the boy studied the broken tree, but not truly. It was just a place to put their eyes while they waited, because there was nothing else to do. They waited. It might have been a day or more, and then the air moved, not all of it, not all at once. It was like a wave, or the ripple from a wave, bending the air for only an instant, and she looked at Billy, and he looked at her and nodded.

— · —

ANDY Cotterman was more than half an hour late and trotting through a fallow field of the Wenslow farm and across that to a dirt road, and then on to the scarred land where three homes were being built. The knock of hammers and high whine of a saw came to him as he hurried, jogging with his hands in his jacket pockets, elbows winged out, eyes ahead on the one house that was finished but not yet landscaped. That's where his father would be waiting.

Andy was twenty-four and ran with a muscular ease. He didn't want to disappoint his dad by being late, but there was nothing he could do now except hurry. He couldn't remember where he had left his car, and he jerked his head around toward the road, but didn't see it. He jogged through a broken fence onto land that had been bulldozed and was now littered with the scraps of paper and wood, cement and wire that were always left over from the building of a house. He saw his father standing at the door of the finished home, and he slowed to a walk and waved, but the man didn't see him.

He saw two men of his father's crew framing a porch on the next house, but they didn't look up from their work. His father was standing at the open door of the new home, looking inside, and Andy sent his voice ahead. "Sorry, Dad."

The man didn't turn, and Andy thought he must be angry. He had asked Andy to meet him on the site and have lunch with him so he could walk Andy through the house and show him the details. He said it was the best finish work he had ever done.

"Sorry, Dad. I just couldn't get away from the phone."

His father kept his back to his son, and Andy began to clutch inside, knowing then that he had hurt the man's feelings, and imagining his father's face with no smile for him and the wound showing in his eyes, and he sighed, taking the last ten steps. "I'm really sorry."

His father turned, and his look was more disturbing than Andy had expected because the man never settled his eyes on him at all, but only shook his head and began walking toward his truck.

"Dad. God." He trailed after his father. "I couldn't just walk away from the paper with all those phone calls." But the man never paused, reaching his truck and pulling open the door. "Wait. Dad!"

Andy's father entered the cab of his truck and closed the door and started the engine, and Andy shouted over the ragged revving of the old Ford. "You're not even going to talk to me? I can't even explain?" But the truck pulled away, and Andy followed it a few steps, his own anger rising, and in the shaking of his head and in the furrowed intensity of his face, he showed to anyone who might be looking how closely he resembled his father, but no one was looking, the framers not pausing in their work or turning their heads, even as Andy sent a last shout after the truck like an arrow. "Dad!"

He looked down the hill from the building site, wondering again where he had parked, thinking there was nothing to do now but to drive to his parents' home and face the man's anger, wondering why his father was taking it so hard.

He set out toward the road and was so knotted over the problem of his father that he had no memory of finding his car and driving it, but found himself walking on Sutter Street, angling across the lawns, noticing that there was a police car in the driveway of his parents' home, parked behind his father's truck.

He jogged toward the open front door of the house, and then he was inside the living room, feeling as if he were under water. It wasn't just the falling darkness as he came in out of the bright sun, it was the muffling of the voices, which he strained to hear, and it was the weight of the air itself. He could almost see the air, and he noticed, by their posture, that it was pressing on his parents, who sat on the sofa, and on his sister, who was kneeling on the floor, and even on the bent neck and shoulders of the tall police officer, whom he knew, Ed Fontaine, whom he had played basketball with in high school and had been an usher at his wedding, and here was Ed in his police uniform in the middle of the living room, staring at the carpet with a face of pain.

Andy felt panic rising in him like poison, and he opened his mouth and moved his eyes to each of them. He could tell that his mother was weeping by the shaking of her body, but he couldn't hear her, and when he took a step closer, he found himself outside again, out on the lawn. There was Ed Tramer, a neighbor, coming across the street and walking by him, his face grave, his body oppressed even here, in the air and the sunlight, and when he passed, Andy felt a great distance between them that he didn't understand.

There was someone else, standing in the street and staring at him. No one else had looked at him, not his father at the building site, not anyone in the house, not the passing neighbor, but this girl was looking at him, and he knew her, vaguely, and then he knew her for certain because he had written the story about her in the newspaper and studied her photograph.

She was Emily Bridger, and she was dead. When he realized this, he was no longer in the yard of his parents' home. He was at the edge of the highway, near a massive trailer truck that was half in a ditch, only its fender smashed, and there was a tow truck and a police car, and the pavement was littered with glass and bits of metal, and a twisted, monstrous version of his own car was in the opposite ditch, and he couldn't look at any of this, and so he jogged away, thrusting his fists into his jacket, and his head shaking vainly as memory flooded through him like blood, instead of blood.

He didn't remember stopping, but he was sitting now by a broken fence in a fallow field, and Emily Bridger was sitting on the ground ten feet away, still watching him. Emily asked him a question, realizing as she spoke the words, that it was the same question Billy Nester had asked her. "Do you know where you are?"

Andy studied his father's building site on the next hill, hearing the hammers knocking out of rhythm. They sounded farther away than they should have. He nodded.

"You know who I am?" Emily asked.

He nodded again, and then he turned to her. "Emily Bridger. You smashed up your car…three weeks ago."

"Three weeks!" She stared hard at her thoughts. "I thought it was just a few days."

He looked at her a long time, and then looked at himself sitting cross-legged on the weedy earth, at his hands limp on his knees, and then he gripped his knees, feeling his fingers pressing through the cloth, and then he rubbed his knees for a full minute, thinking hard, the effort showing on his furrowed face, before he looked at Emily again and asked his own question. "What happens now?"

Emily shrugged.

"You don't know?" He said this with some intensity, and she asked if he was mad at her, and he sighed and looked away and shook his head, thinking aloud now. "My dad couldn't see me. That's why. Couldn't even see me."

"You went all the way inside your house," Emily said. "That was brave."

"I didn't know."

"Truck hit your car, right? That big truck?"

Andy nodded. "Came right at me. Came right into my lane, just drifted right in front of me. God." Saying that word made him look at Emily again. "What about... What's this supposed to be?"

"I don't know what it's supposed to be. I don't know anything. There are more people here. Billy Nester. Remember him?"

Andy nodded slowly, but he was busy thinking. He stood up, and in rising shifted his place again, standing now at the edge of the highway where he had been killed, but there were no longer any trucks or cars there, only some glass left in the ditch and oil stains on the pavement. "Time's gone by," he said, and Emily, beside him, nodded, staring at him. "I used to see you around," she said. "When you came back from college. I used to see you at the A&W for a while."

Andy was still studying the accident scene. "I moved to

Libertyville," he said. "I'm on the paper there." They both realized, after he said it, that he had used the present tense, but neither one mentioned it. "Damn," he said, thinking of the vast panorama that he had believed was his future, seeing it all tumbling together, adventures and women and children and foreign cities all tumbling down. "Damn."

"Sorry." Emily remembered speaking with some of the girls about Andy Cotterman, some of the other senior girls who had decided to have a crush on him. She had decided, after a while, to have one, too, when she saw him dining in his car at the A&W drive-in, and smiling at the waitress, and then he smiled at her and Laurentina Aguilar, a friendly smile, not flirting, but she guessed he wouldn't remember that and so didn't mention it. "You want to meet Billy Nester?" she asked him.

He nodded one of his thoughtful nods, thinking hard again so that there was a slight squint to his dark eyes. "Sure."

"There's an old man, too. Crazy, I think. And here's Billy."

They were in the woods, and Andy did not remember moving, but he stood among the trees with Emily and saw the boy watching them from twenty feet away.

"He stayin'?" Billy asked, and Emily said, "I think so."

Andy said hello and told the boy he remembered him. Everyone in Indian Lake remembered Billy Nester, even if they had never seen him, and they thought of him now as billynester, not as an individual, but as an occurrence, a drowning in their lake, a warning to their children, a tragedy.

"Five years, Billy," Andy said, "and you don't know what's supposed to happen?"

"How do ya know somethin's supposed to happen?"

Andy sighed and did his head-shaking again and said, "Damn" again. "What about the old man?"

"Fegg," Billy said. "Don't know his first name. Forty-some years, he says he's been here…"

"Forty!" Andy walked in a small circle and rubbed his head. He closed his eyes then, feeling his fingertips on his scalp as he rubbed and thought about the truth of this and the puzzle of it.

"How'd you come here?" Billy asked him.

"Crashed his car," Emily said. "Big trailer truck," and to Andy she said, "This is my place. Here."

And they were now standing before Emily's scarred birch, and Andy was nodding. He had stood here before and stared at the same tree, when tire marks and glass and pieces of auto-mobile were still scattered about, just before he wrote the story, and he remembered standing here and thinking about the girl and looking at her photos, imagining a life stopped suddenly in the middle of a breath or a scream, but never imagining this. "Why are we here?" he asked.

He wasn't expecting them to answer but Emily said, "It's just…where we come," and Andy shook his head, unaccepting.

"You been to town?" he asked them.

"I used to go near it," Billy said. "Didn't like it," and Emily said that she had tried it, but somehow, she could only go so far, and then she'd be back where she started, but she had walked all the streets she could walk and even stood outside her home.

"And it's just us?" Andy asked.

"And Fegg."

Andy was shaking his head again. He sat on a fallen tree and thought about his family, about the scene in the living room, and he felt sorry for them and sorry for himself, and he wondered, for a moment, who would write the story of his death, and he began writing it in his mind, and then he looked at the others and said, "How can it be just us? People die all the time. Forty years? There'd be hundreds of people here."

"We don't know, Andy," Emily said, and she sat on the ground in her usual place and stared at her tree. Andy watched her and then sat beside her, and in a moment Billy sat with them, too.

"Can't be," Andy said mostly to himself. "Can't be just us. There'd be people here from…far back. Jesus, there'd be Indians here! From way before, before there was any town."

"What Indians?" Billy asked.

"The Potawatomi Indians. Why d'you think they call it Indian Lake? Didn't your teachers tell you?"

"I only got to the goddamn sixth grade, Andy!"

"There'd be dead people all around!"

Andy was staring at the ground as if the answers might be there among the weeds, but then noticed a small, plain brown bird come to ground and walk about and touch its beak among the grasses, and Andy suddenly clapped his hands, but his palms struck without much sound, and the bird paid no attention, and then it was night, and he wondered how the darkness had eased in unnoticed, like a thief stealing the light while they stood watch.

"I want to talk to the old man," he said.

The girl and the boy looked at him, and Emily, her red-brown hair lit by the light of the half moon, swung her head in a direction into the trees and said, "I saw him over there."

"No, he usually stays at the lumber yard," Billy said. "His house used to be there."

Andy was nodding, deciding to wait for daylight, and he sighed, settling in for the wait, but by the time he finished his sigh, the dawn was coming in among the trees like water bleeding into paper, spreading quickly, and he shivered because he was in the woods at sunrise and he ought to be cold, but it was only memory that tightened and shook his body.

When they reached the lumber yard, Billy thrust his chin upward, pointing, and they saw Fegg seated on the roof of the building. Emily said, "He scares me," and she noticed that he was barefoot, as before, and wearing his threadbare plaid flannels, and his hair was as riotous as ever, but it wasn't any longer, and it would never grow longer and never fall out, and the thought made her touch her own hair, checking it and finding it the same, not mussed, not dirty, just the same. The old man was already talking to them, but they couldn't hear him.

"Why is he on the roof?" Andy asked.

"Says he's got the view from there that he used to get from his bedroom window: the woods and a little bit of the lake. He'll be down here."

And then Fegg was walking toward them, coming close and talking, and no one had noticed his descent from the roof. "What the hell you doing here, and who the hell is this one? Another new one, another goddamn new one to bother me and crowd the place and get in my eyes and make me look at his face, and I don't want to look at your stupid face in my view, get it out, get yourself out and stay in your own place. This is my place, and who do you think you are, coming here? Who in the hell do you suppose you are compared to me and..."

"Wait," Andy said.

"...to what happened to me, and you think I'm going to waste my eyes on you?"

"Why are we here?"

"What?!"

"What are we doing here?" Andy asked, and while the old man with the gray, stabbing eyes was silent, he added, "I'm Andy Cotterman, and I just came..."

"I don't give two shits who you are!" Fegg came closer, his lips snarling away from his almost toothless mouth. "I'm not talking to you. I'm not wasting my breath on some stupid ass, 'cause I don't have any breath! My breath was taken away from me and my view was taken away by a goddamn pillow that was big as the whole world and it was the last goddamn thing I saw; and before she put it on me she looked like God; she looked like she knew everything and made up her mind and her mind was God and all the goddamn judgment in the world; and she was glad and she was God and she was killing me like the end of the world and I saw pillow for the rest of my life and I heard shoutin', and it was her shoutin' like she was God and I was a sinner 'cause I called her names and told her what the hell to do and she was *supposed* to do that, supposed to 'cause I was sick and she wasn't sick and she could go up and down and outside and piss and shit on her own and I couldn't so the hell with her and all the names and all what I said and whatever I said to her, 'cause I was old and sick and couldn't work and couldn't have her anymore and couldn't hit her anymore 'cause my arms got thin and I had arms once and I had legs that were thick and got thin and to hell with her and with you, with your little goddamn life and your puny little years, you goddamn kid, all you goddamn kids don't amount to me, not to me, not to a man that…"

"Shut up!" Andy advanced into the old face, just an inch from the man's nose and shouted again, "Shut up! You stupid son of a bitch!"

Fegg's mouth was as wide open as his fierce and unbelieving eyes as Andy gathered his fists and trembled with rage and screamed his words like sharp claws at the old man, taking a step so that Fegg had to move a step back.

"You're not more than me! You're not more than me, you dumb old asshole! You're not more than me! You were almost dead anyway, you mean old piece of shit! I'm twenty-four goddamn years old and I was going to be the managing editor of the goddamn *Lake County Post*—next year! And I was going to move to a Chicago paper, a Chicago paper! And I had a car and I had an apartment with my own things, my own things, and my friends! And I was up to a hundred push-ups a day, and I was learning the goddamn guitar, and I was going to play it when me and my friends had parties at the lake! And I was going to a party; I was going to a party Saturday with Kidda Weems, with Kidda Weems, and she's beautiful, and she said yes, she said

sure, and I was going to kiss her and I was going to touch her
and I was going to touch women and make love to women and
I was going to travel, just pack a kit and travel maybe to Turkey,
to goddamn Istanbul, goddamn Madagascar, and write about
it for a paper and I was going to swim in every ocean of the
world and maybe I'd get married and I'd be a father you stupid
selfish old bastard — except this truck, this truck came out of its
lane and hit me and I'll never do it, never do it, never, but I'm
not going to wait around here for no reason; I'm not going to
wait around here and listen to your self-pitying crap about your
goddamn pillow! We all have a goddamn pillow! We all have
a goddamn pillow!"

Only Fegg's throat moved, the knobby apple bobbing as
he swallowed, and then he turned and walked away, muttering
what couldn't be heard, and then he was on top of the roof
again, after only a few steps, and Andy watched him up there,
and saw that he was staring at the view over the woods to the
lake and still muttering on.

Billy and Emily were watching Andy. They looked at each
other, acknowledging what they had just seen and heard, and
then turned back to Andy again, studying him as he studied
the old man. Emily was deciding that she would continue her
crush on Andy Cotterman, and it would be her last crush and
last forever, she supposed. Andy turned then and caught her
staring at him, she felt her face warm and wondered if it
was still possible to blush, and then they were all back at Andy's
place, at the roadside ditch along the highway where he died,
Andy sitting cross-legged, and Billy standing with his thin arms

folded, and Emily sitting beside Andy, her legs skewed to the side because of her skirt.

Billy felt he couldn't breathe right, like his breath, or the memory of his breath, was shaking on its passage through his chest, because there were painful words making their way through his thin chest. "At least you got to grow up," he said to Andy, and Andy looked at him, wondering if it might be worse to stop at eleven, and then he turned back to the road and the fading oil stains on the pavement.

"Not enough," Andy said.

And Billy said again, "Well…at least you got to grow up!"

"What did you want to be?" Emily asked the boy, to divert him from his anger, "if you…grew up?"

"Taller," Billy said. "Stronger. Strong enough to beat the hell out of my brothers or at least keep 'em from pushing me around."

"Did you ever think of…some kind of work?" she asked.

He shrugged and said, "Airplanes, maybe. Flyin' 'em."

She nodded, thinking about this until she noticed that both Billy and Andy were staring at her, waiting.

"I worked part-time at Barbara's Beauty Salon. She was training me, but I didn't really like it. And she let me go 'cause I didn't talk enough to the customers. I couldn't make conversation, so she said she had to let me go." She stared at Andy then. "I had it in my mind to talk to your sister, about nursing school. I almost did once. I bet it's hard, though."

"She likes it," Andy said. "It's hard, but she likes it. I bet you would have been good at it."

She let her stare linger on him. "Why?"

"Because you're kind."

She swallowed and felt like she might begin to cry, but she didn't, and she was glad, hearing him say that, and she held on to it, to his face and his words to her. She would keep that always in this forever they seemed to share.

They were quiet then, and Andy began absently fingering the weeds in the ditch as he studied the memory of his accident, and Emily watched him, and they were all silent for what could have been a week, and then Andy said, "Fegg's pillow was a pillow, and mine was a truck. What was your pillow, Emily? Your car? Something wrong with your car?"

She tightened and looked away and didn't answer, and he didn't stop staring at the highway and fingering weeds, but he said, after a while, "I know you crashed that car once before, almost a year before."

"I broke my wrist that time," she said, her mouth feeling dry, "that's all. How did you know about that?"

"I wrote about you, in the paper. I wrote about the accident when you died, too. I talked to your parents."

"You did?" Her voice was weakening.

"Was it something wrong with the steering?"

"Is that what my parents said?"

"Your dad thought that might have been it."

Emily stared at Andy now, waiting until he turned and met her eyes, and then she swallowed or tried to swallow, and she asked, "What did *you* think?"

He looked at her a while before speaking, weighing his words. "I had the feeling…that you wanted to do it."

Her eyes began to burn and blink, and she knew she'd be

crying if she were alive, and Andy said, "I just had that feeling, and I thought to myself…if it's true…I'll never know why."

"You won't," she said, and her voice cracked and she felt the old sickness move through her body.

Billy said to her, "You *meant* to? You killed *yourself*?"

Emily stood and left them just by beginning the motion, and she was gone, and they knew she'd be at her place, by her tree, and Billy began a movement to follow her, but Andy said, "Leave her alone now," and Billy stopped.

"Wow," Billy said. "Did it to herself. On purpose! Why?"

"What about you, Billy?"

"What?"

"What happened at the lake? Why don't you take anybody to your place, to the lake?"

"I don't go there."

"Why not?" But Billy left, and Andy was alone, fingering through the weeds, and staring now at one slender stalk and gripping it to pull it from its fragile clutch on the earth, but his fingers slipped off, and he tried again and again, but he could not tighten his fingers on the stem and pull it out. He could not kill the weed.

—·—

IN the home of the Cottermans, autumn was passing slowly and with great effort, like a journey through deep mud. It was eight days since Andy's death, and then it was, finally, ten, and then on the fourteenth day the Cottermans began to count in weeks.

Because Andy had lived away from home for a year in Libertyville, they had no issues with setting the table for three or watching television without him or with not hearing his voice or his steps in the house, but his room had never been changed, because four times within the past year he had come to visit and stayed for the weekend or over the Christmas holiday, so his bed was always made and ready, and some of his old clothes still waited for him in the dresser drawers and in the closet.

His sister's room was down the hall beyond the shared bathroom. She was nineteen, studying nursing and working as an aid at the hospital in McHenry, and she couldn't sleep through the night because she would come half awake and feel so strongly that Andy was in his room that she would, against all reason, have to get up and walk into her brother's bedroom and see, and the silent, empty weightlessness of that unoccupied space would hang sorrow on her like a heavy coat, and she could not sleep for fits of quiet weeping.

She began sleeping in Andy's room, so that when she awoke, she'd have nowhere to go and could stay in the bed and look only once into the darkness and then give herself to sleep again, and this plan worked for her so that she passed day fifteen and day twenty-eight without the stunning exhaustion that had embraced her.

Andy's mother, who had been known as a quiet person, found some ease in releasing a river of words about Andy as a boy and as a young man, so that people close to her began to hold back their sympathies and their own memories of her son for fear of the flood that would keep them adrift for up to half an hour at a time, while Burt, Andy's father, became much more reticent and began spending more and more time in the one finished house of his small development, the house where he had waited to meet his son, and he would walk through the place, speaking to his son in his mind, pretending that Andy had come that day and constructing what he would have said to him as he showed him the wainscoting and the molding and the details on the built-in shelves, and constructing what Andy would have said in return, and even shaping the expressions on his son's face as they went through the house and then stood at the truck and had their sandwiches and drinks and spoke of other things and laughed together as their lives rolled on without any calamitous interruption, and all this while Andy, or the remnant of Andy, the still-Andy consciousness that was invisible to all of them, stood outside in the yard or sometimes entered his old room late in the silent nights or walked in the forest or through parts of the town or remained at the place beside the highway where he had been killed by a truck.

In the home of the Nesters, the five years since Billy's death had softened the random shocks that used to come with the setting of the table, one place less, and the doing of the laundry by Mrs. Nester without the small clothes of her youngest and with the lack of his bike in the yard and with the sight of him in the old photos, often blurred because he was never without motion until the day he was pulled so cold and so blue and so irrevocably still from the water. Since that day not his father, his mother, or even his nineteen-year-old brother, Chick, whose friends partied there all summer, ever went to the lake.

In the home of the Bridgers, Emily's mother was waging a guerrilla war against Emily's father, a conflict without major battles, but with sniping and booby traps and the occasional raid. The war had started soon after Emily's life had crashed against a birch tree seven weeks ago. Since then her mother had never touched a piece of clothing, a magazine, a comb that had belonged to her daughter, and Emily had been a messy girl. Her father avoided these things, even avoided looking at them as much as possible, and he wept more than his wife and kept to his lounge chair in the living room or his bed. His broken back had made him a housebound man since a fall from a ladder six years ago when he had been an electrician, and he had suffered from depression all of these years.

When he could no longer stand the sight of Emily's sweater twisted into a corner of the sofa, he asked his wife, "Why don't you move that?"

And she looked up from her work at the living room desk and said, "Because I want you to do it," and then she watched him, her eyes into him like fishhooks. "I want to see you touch it," she said, but he couldn't, and when he tilted his chair forward and struggled to rise, she didn't help him. He rose as straight as he could and walked with his canes to the bedroom, and she watched him all the way, saying, just before he was out of her sight, "Why can't you? Why can't you?" her face telling him that she knew why he couldn't, and that she knew everything.

While her father was taking his halting walk to his bedroom, carrying in his back the sharp barbs of his wife's stare, the remnant of his dead daughter, Emily, was across the street, watching the house and wondering about the life of her parents beyond the windows and the door. She could not come any closer because she felt that the sickness was still alive in there, and it repelled her like the smell of something rotten, a mixture of guilt and shame and anger and loss that was still poison, even to the dead.

Once when she had used the limit of her courage and attempted to cross her yard to her door, she had been pushed away by the same irresistible shove one magnet gives to another, and she had found herself back at her tree. She had the same experience when she tried to walk to her friend Laurentina's home in Indian Hill, and in this way, she discovered the borders of her world, about two miles in any direction from its nucleus, the location of her death.

She found, too, that living people felt more and more foreign to her, residents of another country with another language, and she never studied them, moving at this moment through a flock of boys on bikes as if they were swift sparrows who never even caught her eye, but she was halted by the sight of a familiar face, a girl she knew well, and found herself excited, found herself moving quickly—and was suddenly beside the girl who was marching along at a pace.

Her name was Nancy Darrow, the younger sister of one of Emily's best friends. Nancy was twelve or so and moving down the gravel road with purpose. Emily walked beside her, staring, and then pretending the girl could hear her. "Hi, Nancy. Where you going? How's Cathy these days? Is she still seeing Matt Patterson? Did he pin her? Do you feel me hear near you, Nancy? Nancy?"

The girl made no sign that she heard or sensed Emily's

presence, as she moved along steadily, focused, intent about something.

"Where you going? What are you thinking so hard about?" She had known Nancy since the girl was eight years old, and even then was certain that she was going to be a teacher like her mother, and she was sticking to it, at twelve years old now, telling anyone who asked her about the future. Was she upset, Emily wondered? "Nancy look at me. Look at me. What's worrying you? Are you thinking about me? Does Cathy miss me? Do you? Do you miss our talks? I'm right here, you know. *Do* you know? Can you…?"

Nancy turned to enter the yard of a small, old house and walked the gravel path to the front step and Emily joined her there. "You have a friend here? Is it…?" Nancy knocked on the edge of the screen door, which was opened by a girl her own age, who made a small smile and swung the door for Nancy to enter. "Are you two going to study?" Nancy made a swift smile at the girl and was serious again, moving into the house where Emily could not follow. "Is everything all right? Why…?"

But Emily was left with her questions and moved to the nearest window, not to look inside, but to study herself in the glass, to see if she carried the same troubled look as Nancy, but she didn't, and she wondered if that intensity was a normal look for the two girls, if that was the look of a crowded life, or if that was a look of life itself.

She turned from the window and was held still by the sight of one of her own as she watched Andy cross the road a block away.

She moved close to him with the same effort as thought, now trailing a few steps behind him as he pounded along, his steps as soundless as her own, but his legs pumping with a sense of hurry, and his hands in his jacket pockets, head held upright and shoulders stiff. She was worried for him, worried by his impatience. It reminded her of Nancy, as if Andy wasn't fully dead but only waiting for something unknown, driven by this waiting, and it showed in his troubled face even as he smiled at her, turning around to wait for her. His smile was on and off like a bulb, and then they were walking together, and she was trying to keep up with his stride.

"Been outside your home?" he asked her.

"Uh-huh. You, too?"

"Been all over. Far as I can go."

"Did you go inside?" Andy was the only one of them who could enter his home. He would walk toward it at night when it was very still and approach the door, and then he would be inside, but only in his old room, because it was the one place that would accept him, and he would stand in his room, among the dresser and desk and bed he had grown up with and look at the wallpaper and the framed photographs of aircraft and sometimes look out the window at the view he had stared at a thousand times as a boy, and he would feel the sleep of his family, the slow, even breathing, but last night he had been surprised and stayed for only what he would have called two seconds when he used to count by the clock.

"I don't think I should go in anymore. My sister's sleeping in my room now. I don't know why, but... There's nothing to learn in there, anyway. Nothing that helps me understand. I wish I could hear them, really hear them."

"I don't."

"Don't you want to find out?"

Emily shrugged, moving along beside him and now and then looking at the side of his face, while he kept eyes ahead on the puzzle of his thoughts. "So, this is okay for you?" he asked. "All this waiting around, for what? For years? That's okay?"

She shrugged again, and that stopped him, and they halted and stared, and she felt sympathy for him because of the trouble that was always darkening his face, and because, underneath it, he seemed like a lost boy, and she wanted to comfort him. "How can that be okay?" he asked her, not angry, but desperate to understand.

"I don't know, Andy. Maybe because…this is better than my life."

"This?" He studied her words as if they still hung in the air between them. "Is it? Really?"

She nodded.

"But you won't tell me why, will you?"

She only looked down, her silence answering him.

"So you're not sorry you killed yourself?"

"You know," she said, trying to slow the pace of the conversation, "you scare Billy."

"Why?"

"All your questions. That's why he's been staying away."

"What's wrong with questions? What's wrong with wanting to know? I need to figure it out. I need to, Emily."

"I know."

"Don't you have any questions?"

She looked at her shoes and nodded, and he waited. She kept him waiting, wanting to ease him away from his hurry. "I want to know if you're in love with Kidda Weems." At least she created a small smile on his face, briefly creasing through the trouble there.

"Kidda Weems. No, I like her. I asked her out."

"Sure you did. She's beautiful and Miss Lake County and all that."

"She's runner-up," he said, "but I never got a chance to know her or love her or really love any girl."

"But she's the one you wanted."

He shrugged. "There was a party, and I asked her. I could've asked somebody else. I would've asked you, but you were dead."

She laughed then. Even inside his trouble, he could still make her laugh. "You wouldn't have asked me."

"Why not? I remember seeing you—at the A&W, in the next car. I remember seeing you smile at me and thinking, that's a pretty girl; wonder who she is?"

"You remember that?"

He nodded, and they walked on together, but more slowly. "Your napkin fell off your tray," she said. "When the waitress brought the food to your car, the napkin blew off, and nobody saw it but me, and after she left, I was going to get out of the car and pick it up and give it to you."

"I wish you had," he said. "Why didn't you?"

She shrugged again. "Shy, and…" The memory of tears

suddenly thickened in her throat, and then they were at her tree. She was sitting at the scarred trunk of her birch, leaning her back against it, and Andy sat beside her and also leaned on the tree, only inches away from her shoulder. A truck went by on the highway, and they didn't hear it, but felt the earth hum with its passage. Emily pressed her back against the rough scars of her killing tree and felt the sickness rise in her, hot and rancid.

"I was afraid to go with boys," she said. "I wanted to, but I was afraid, and it made me feel sick. I wanted a boy to touch me and me to touch him, not a particular boy, but sometimes I imagined a particular boy, and once I imagined my teacher, Mr. Kiner, 'cause he was nice and funny and I liked him, and after the A&W, I imagined you a couple of times, but it always ended up making me feel sick because that's what my father did, and he always said that it was for him to do and nobody else and nobody would understand but it was just for me and him and it made us special, that we had something so special, and he would come into my room at night or real early in the morning when my mom was still asleep and he would take the covers down and stand there and touch me or sometimes kneel like he was praying, kneel next to the bed and touch me all over, since I was, I don't know, eleven, maybe once or twice a week since I was eleven or twelve, and I was scared, but I liked that he was there, having a secret time with me, and it was the only time anybody said they loved me, so I liked that part and I hated it, too, some of the touching, and he'd stop for a while, for months, but then he'd start again, and I liked it and hated it, hated it more, but I couldn't tell anybody because I was so ashamed and because he begged me, and even my mother, when I would start, when I would start to even think about telling her, she would walk away, and I knew she didn't love me anymore, and she stopped looking at me, because she knew, or she was afraid to know, to know for sure, and I couldn't let anyone touch me because I felt dirty and I was going to leave, I knew I had to leave, and I graduated school and I got to be eighteen, and I didn't leave; I didn't leave; I didn't leave, so I killed myself because I felt so bad, and now I think, sometimes I think, what if I had stepped out of Laurentina Aguilar's car at the A&W that night and picked up your napkin and you had talked to me and we had gotten to know each other, maybe it would've been different, but I don't think so, because I felt so sick, but it's different now, because we're together, at least this way, and I don't feel so sick anymore."

She covered her mouth with her hands and remembered how crying felt, but there were no tears, only a shuddering in her chest and stomach. She rolled away from the tree so she could lie fully on the leafy ground, and she drew up her legs, and her breath came in shudders, too, or was it only the remembering? She wasn't sure.

When she opened her eyes, she saw that Andy was lying beside her, facing her, their noses only a few inches apart as if they were lying in bed together, and they stared a long time, and then he said, "Thanks for the napkin."

She was confused, and then she smiled and felt her smile

shake, or the memory of that, and she said in a broken voice, "Sure."

"What's your name?"

"Emily Bridger."

"I'm Andy Cotterman. Please don't kill yourself."

"Okay."

"Move out of the house."

"All right."

"And stay alive."

"Okay."

"I wish I could ask you to a party."

"Ask me."

"Emily, there's a party at Long Lake this Saturday. Will you come with me?"

"I can't."

"Why not?"

"I'm dead."

"That's okay."

They laughed, then, quietly, stopping and then starting again, not so quietly, and not being able to stop as she wept within the laughter, and they used their memories to touch each other's faces as the remembrance of tears shined her smile.

Billy heard them and came to the tree, kneeling just six feet from them and watching them, enjoying their laughter and made sad by it because he was outside of it, and because he hadn't laughed that way for all the long while of his death. The laughing couple on the ground couldn't see him, but Emily knew he was there, because when they quieted, she said, "Tell him, Billy."

"Tell him what?"

"Whatever you can," she said. "Whatever you know. It feels all right, telling."

And Andy said to the boy, "If we tell everything, maybe we'll figure it all out, why we're here, what to do."

"You still think there's something we're supposed to do."

Andy said, "Yes" with certainty.

And Emily said, "Tell him about the other ones who come," and that made Andy turn and stare eagerly at the boy. Billy sat sullen, with his thin arms wrapping his knees, but Andy's eyes were ropes, and the boy felt the strong pulling in his mind.

"Some come for a while," the boy said, "but they don't stay. Sometimes it's just a few minutes, sometimes it feels like a day or two, but I don't like it. I don't like to look at them if they're not going to stay, 'cause they can't see you. Their eyes are dead like, and empty. They're not ready to be here, and I don't like being around 'em and watching 'em, 'cause for years, I'd watch, and I'd hope they'd be here with me, that they'd stay, and they never did until Emily. There's one here now."

"Now? Where?"

And then they were moving out of the woods and across the highway, and without walking they were standing in the back yard of the Groff house, and the back door was open except for the screen, and behind the screen was Mrs. Groff, a heavy woman of about fifty who had been sick for years and used a wheelchair. Emily and Andy both remembered seeing her in town, wheeled by her husband or her sister, but Billy had died before the diabetes had struck her down, and now she was dead, and the remnant of her stood at the back door of her house and looked through the screen at the yard and the three plum trees, but didn't see them, didn't seem to absorb anything she saw, and her mouth was slack, like the stained blue cotton gown that hung on her swollen body.

"How do you know she won't stay?" Andy asked him, and Billy walked toward Mrs. Groff, and they followed, and they all stopped just five feet from the door. "Her edges," Billy said, and they saw how she wasn't fully formed, and when she moved her head, they saw a double exposure, an image in one place and the memory of an image in another. Light came through her. "She's already goin'," Billy said. "See?"

The others stared at the woman, and Billy said, "That means she's goin'," and they watched her become more light than flesh or gown or hair, not bright light, just the light of the day penetrating her. They stayed the whole time and watched, and she never said a word and never saw them, and then she was more not there than there, and then she was gone. Billy hadn't watched this in years, watched the whole coming and going, and it shook him, and he was moving away, and they followed and found themselves where they had never been taken by the boy. They were at the lake.

Indian Lake is a ragged circle except for one extension that has always been called the Bend, and in the bend of the lake is a pier, an old, unstable wooden pier that runs twenty feet into the water, and on shore there is a wide grassy bank that inclines gradually upwards from the pier. The Bend has always been a choice for fishermen or for small groups who want to swim away from the crowded sandy beach, and Billy was sitting far up on the top of the incline as Andy and Emily arrived, and they sat on either side of the boy as he looked out over the Bend, which was empty of people now as autumn was being chilled slowly on its way into an unrelenting Illinois winter.

Andy's crash site still showed oil stains on the pavement and bits of glass in the weeds of the highway ditch, and Emily's tree showed the scarring of her crash, but Billy's place of death was serene and unmarked.

They waited a long time for the boy to speak, and then he said, "We were on the pier."

"You and your brothers," Andy said, familiar with the story, and the boy nodded and was silent again, and it was difficult for Andy to wait because he wanted to have all of the information and to pick through it for clues.

And then Billy said, "They threw me in." And this exploded the lore of Billy Nester's death into a fine dust. "For a joke," Billy said, staring at the pier, his hands beginning to rub his thin arms out of a growing nervousness and out of the memory of his old cold death, "'cause I was bothering 'em. They always... They never wanted to take me, but I... Anyway, I couldn't swim. They knew that. I was talkin' and they grabbed me in the middle of talkin' and threw me far off the pier, and I hit the water, and it's deep off the pier, so I couldn't touch." He rubbed his arms furiously, and then stood but kept himself wrapped in his own embrace and kept his eyes on the water. "And I could hear 'em yellin' and laughin', and I was…tryin'… I swallowed water, and…" He walked about without direction, gripping his upper arms now and shaking his head as the memory stung him like a following of wasps. "They knew I couldn't swim… I never… I didn't go in over my head. I didn't like the water at all, didn't like the mud on the bottom, so I hardly ever… 'Dogpaddle!'" he yelled suddenly, and Emily and Andy were on their feet, and Emily went to the boy, but he kept moving. "'Dogpaddle! Dogpaddle, you jerk!' I heard 'em yellin' and laughin', and then I sank down into the weeds and the goddamn mud. I hated that slimy mud. 'Dogpaddle!'" On this final, furious shout, his voice broke, and he sat down suddenly, facing away from the water. Emily sat beside him, but the boy turned away from her and sent Andy his glance as if throwing a sharp stone, his face contorted. "So what good is it rememberin'? Huh? And talkin'! You still think there's somethin' we're supposed to do?"

Andy said quietly, "Yes."

"What? Huh? What's supposed to happen? Nothing!"

"They lied," Andy said. "Did you know your brothers lied?"

Billy looked at his lap, at his bare legs beyond the baggy trunks, at his body that would never grow older and he shook his head.

Andy came closer. "They said they were walking away from the lake when they heard you dive in. They said you dived."

"I figured they'd probably lie to stay out of trouble. They always lied."

"They said they ran back and jumped in and tried to find you, but they found you too late."

"Maybe they did. Maybe they tried to save me. They probably did."

Andy sat beside him, as close as Emily, as close as possible without touching because they couldn't touch. If they moved close enough to touch and didn't feel the touching, it shook them, so they learned to come as close as possible. "Do you know about your brothers? Now?"

"I see Chick workin' at Kosloski's gas station. I used to go near the house, but once I made my mother cry."

"You mean…?" Andy looked beyond Billy and met Emily's eyes. Then they both stared at the boy again, and Andy asked, "She saw you?"

Billy shrugged his bony shoulders. "She was hangin' up clothes, and I just stood there a while, and she stopped, and then started cryin' and went inside. She didn't look at me. So… I don't go back. I never see Joey, even on the road."

"Your brother Joey joined the Marines. He's one of our Korean vets," Andy said, and then realized Billy didn't know about Korea. "It was a war," he said. "He's still in the Marines."

Billy was nodding, eyes on his lap. "I think Chick saw me once."

"Saw you? Really saw you?" Andy asked, and the boy shrugged again and said, "I was hangin' around the gas station, watchin' him. I used to just…watch 'em, my brothers, when I was alive, to learn stuff, 'cause they never talked to me much, and I was there with Chick, a long time after I was dead, maybe last year; I don't know, watchin' him change the tires on a car, just to be doin' somethin', just to be near him, and he seemed pissed off, like he always was, and then he stood up with the lug wrench in his hand, and I was behind him, and I think he saw me in the car window, my reflection. He just stood there, real stiff, and then he broke the window with the lug wrench—just where my face was, at least I think where my face was, and it was just like he was sayin' 'stay the hell away from me,' like he always said, so the hell with him, the bastard. I don't go near 'im now."

"I didn't think they could see us," Emily said. "Nobody sees me."

"Me neither," Billy said, but I think my mom knew I was there, and I think Chick knew I was there."

Andy said, "I don't know. Maybe she was just sad, and maybe Chick was just pissed off. I don't know."

"What's the difference?" Billy said. "What the hell difference what you think? I don't care what you think, and I don't care if they saw me or not. What's the difference? It doesn't mean anything about us. You still think there's something to mean about us, something that it all means. So now you know all about me and my dumb, stupid death, so what does it mean? Nothin'."

"Something," Andy said.

And Billy said, "Bullshit."

"Maybe," Emily said.

"Maybe what?" Billy asked.

"*Something*," Andy said, and he said it with such conviction and hope and even pain that his voice forced Emily to rush through her memory.

"Once I thought I saw this man staring at me." She said. "I mean after I died. The old man named Loon, but…"

"The sign painter?" Andy asked, hard focused on her. "Van Loon? He was staring at you?" Andy's eyes were gripping her, rushing her.

"I thought he was, and I walked closer. And he just stood there. He's so tall, and he looked… Some people said he was crazy, and that he saw things that weren't there. I walked right up to him, but…then he was staring just above me. Just… staring so hard…at nothing, I guess, or just…some memory, but…" She had wanted to offer something to Andy, some kind of possibility, even a failed possibility, and this made Billy drag something to the table, something he had left behind.

"When I first came here, somebody saw me for sure, but didn't want to."

Andy aimed his look at Billy and didn't need to speak, his energy burning the boy.

"I don't like to think about it," Billy said.

"Think about it, Billy!"

"You shouldn't…" Emily's voice fell away, and Andy turned his power and tension on her like a harsh light.

"Shouldn't what?"

"Yell at him." She said it softly, but her words made Andy stop and breathe and close his eyes. When he opened them, the heat was gone, but not the desperation.

"Sorry, Billy. Please… Please tell me about somebody seeing you."

"It was Myrna Gresha. You know her?"

"Everybody does," Emily said.

"She's supposed to be…kind of a witch or…." Billy shrugged his thin shoulders, his face dark with the memory.

"She used to find things for people," Emily said. "Not a witch, Billy, but… She had 'the sight' people said. Some people would ask her the future, or…"

"I know," Andy said. "I know all about her. I wrote the story when she came back from prison."

"Nobody talks to her much anymore," Emily said.

Billy asked, "Prison for what?"

Andy answered in a rush. "She found somebody's buried money and kept some for herself. Now tell me. Tell me about her seeing you."

"I was just here a little while and…just walkin' around, trying to get used to it, and nobody ever saw me, but Myrna was across the street one time and stopped and turned and looked right at me. Right at me. So I went over to her, but she was already walkin' away, and I said, 'You see me?' And she wouldn't turn to me again but she said…"

Emily asked, "She said something to you?!" and Andy said, "What? What?!"

"She said, 'Go away now. Just go away'. And she started walkin' faster, and I tried to keep up, and she kinda hissed at me, 'Go away now!' And she hurried right on, and that was all. And I've seen her maybe ten times since then, and she never looks, never, and I used to try to walk with her and talk, but I stopped, 'cause it was just somebody else telling me to get away from 'em, like my brothers, like my dad, too, and other people, so the hell with her, yellin' at me, the hell with her, and she *is* a witch."

"I can't remember where she lives," Andy said, his face hard with concentration as he searched through his mind like a burglar. "Damn! I can't remember her address! Where…?"

"It's far. It's up in Indian Hill someplace," Billy said. "I can't go that far."

"Me neither," Emily said. "I tried—cause my friend Laurentina lives there and I'd really like to see her, but…"

"Where did *you* see her, Billy?" Andy was on his feet.

"I don't know. Kinda near the hardware store that first time. But I've seen her on Idlewild Drive. She cleans houses. I don't know which ones."

Andy turned and was gone. Emily and Billy were silent a while, sitting together, looking at the lake but not seeing it, and, finally, Billy said, "She won't be any help."

"I hope he finds her, though," Emily said. "Just 'cause he's so…upset. I hope she sees him and talks to him."

"And then what?"

"I don't know."

"*You* think there's something that's supposed to happen?"

"I don't know."

Maybe each day and each night stood for only a couple of hours, Andy thought, maybe what felt like two hours equaled twenty-four in this torturous limbo, but just to be sure he walked the length of Idlewild Drive again and again every day, sometimes searching other streets nearby, and once discovering he could walk all the way to Weems Market. He couldn't enter the store, but he could wait and watch outside, and maybe Kidda Weems was working there, and he could watch her if she came in and out and see again how pretty she was and imagine his date with her at the lake if only that truck hadn't come into his lane, but then he thought that seeing her, watching her face and her body would only be the counting of his losses and then the pain and anger would come, and he didn't want to be captured by that. He was determined to keep his mind on the learning and the figuring and finding out the why of being here and the way to move on, to somehow move on, so he did not wait outside Weems Market to see Kidda but walked back to Idlewild Drive, looking for Myrna Gresha.

He worried that if he did see her, he might not recognize her, so he tried to hold the photo in his mind, the picture that ran with his small story of the return of Myrna Gresha to Indian Lake, Illinois, after two years in prison, not a very clear photo. Was she fifty? She was thin, dark. Was she tall? She may have been pretty once. There was no smile.

Then right there, on Idlewild, in the middle of one of the dozens of days dealt to him like cards, she came, stepping out of an old Ford with its chrome rusted or fallen away, leaving holes, giving the auto the appearance of having been strafed.

She carried a plastic bucket with old towels and rags and a cheap, fraying purse, and her plain dress had been washed two hundred times. She had to pause to secure the car door that bounced open every time she closed it, and so Andy was able to walk up behind her, and then begin to say her name, but instead blurted, "What's supposed to happen, Myrna?"

She swore and banged at the door again, and it bounced open again and she stopped and sighed, and Andy repeated, "What's supposed to happen?" and this time the desperation thinned his voice. She slammed the door with both hands while she kicked it, and this time it held, and she moved around the old car to make her way toward the flagstones that led to the Schaefer house, where she would be cleaning today. Andy walked just behind her, and before she reached the steps, he began again. "Please! Myrna! What's supposed to…"

She did not look at him or slow her pace, but she said, in a very strong voice for a thin, small woman, "Andy Cotterman, you just leave me alone now. Leave me alone."

Andy was stunned, and he shouted as she neared the door to the house. *"Please!* What's…"

She rang the doorbell and waited on the stone steps, feeling his stare on her and his wild hope, and she said, with some speck of pity, "Everybody goes. Everybody goes in time."

The door went unanswered, but Myrna opened it and began to enter the house, and now Andy's voice contained tears or the memory of tears. *"No!* No, Myrna. There's Fegg! Forty years!"

She was struggling a bit with all she carried, but half inside now, and her last words snapped at him.

"Everybody goes!" And she was in and the door was closed, and Andy was back by the highway, sitting in the ditch that still held some bits of glass and metal from his fatal crash, and his face was in his hands and his chest shaking. By the time he had gathered himself and dropped his hands and moaned out a sigh of great fatigue, Emily and Billy were sitting near him. It was day, and traffic hummed softly past them like the droning of wasps.

His friends only looked at him until Emily finally asked, "Did you...?" And he nodded.

"I talked to her and she heard me and talked to me. She talked to me! She didn't look at me, didn't want to look at me, but she called me by my name!"

"She did?"

"By your name?!"

"Yes! She said we'd all go. She said everybody goes."

"Where?" they both asked at once.

"I don't know. I don't know! But I tried to tell her it's not true. I wanted to tell her about Fegg, but... Listen... Listen, we have to keep trying. You hear me? We have to!"

"Why?!" Billy shouted, frustrated. "Why do we have to do anything?!"

"So we can understand! So we can figure it out! Why do some come and go, and why do we stay? Why aren't there more of us, a hundred of us?!"

"Maybe there's more." Billy's voice rose to match Andy's. "Maybe there's more but we can't see 'em 'cause they're too far away, way past Indian Hill or way over by the bowling alley, and we can't get to 'em, and they can't get to us!"

"Right here!" Andy shouted this. "Right here, Billy! There would be more! All the dead—in years of time?! It doesn't make sense!"

"Why does it have to make sense?!" Billy's voice was cracking now, tears coming.

"Because it does, Billy! Because there's a reason!"

Billy turned his head away suddenly, so they wouldn't see him weep, and then he was gone. Andy looked at the spot where he had been, and then saw that Emily was staring at him, her eyes sad and full.

"I'm going to…see about him," she said, and Andy nodded to her, sorry he had shouted at the boy, and then he was alone.

Emily tried the inclining bank near the lake's pier, and found Billy, and sat beside him, not sure what to say, and then decided she would wait for him to speak. In a long while he took his eyes from the water and stared at her. "You don't have to be here. You can stay with him."

"Let him try to understand it, Billy. What does it hurt? So what if he does figure it out?"

Billy sniffed, looking at the lake again. "So, he'll figure it out, and what? He'll go. And then you'll go. And what if there's nothin' to figure out about me? I don't want to be here alone again. Just me and that bastard, Fegg."

She moved closer to the boy, as close as she could, and sat another while. "We won't leave you here, Billy. If we go away, we'll all go together. All right?"

After a long moment, the boy began to nod.

— · —

THE home of the Feggs no longer existed, so Chester Fegg sat on the metal roof of the lumber yard building which covered all traces of his home's foundation dating from 1879, and every scrap of what had been his life, so that all he could see now of the past was the view across the road to the trees and the channel and beyond the channel to clustered rooftops and to the lake, and it had all been forest, before the road and the houses, just a forest and a path, and what he stared at from the roof was the memory of a forest and a path and the walking of a woman on the path, a woman coming home, the woman who had finally turned on him and killed him, the one he thought of as the traitorous wife who had taken his voice and his life into a pillow and left him nothing but this roof and this view of a forest and a path and a woman, a young woman, as he saw her, as he remembered her on the path, watching her again and again, ten thousand times, watching her come home in the days when she had loved him.

— · —

IN the home of the Nesters, dinner was mostly silent except for the business of cutting and eating and scraping. Mrs. Nester did have one offering of ambient worry about Joey way out in California and hoping that the Marine base was safe, because he was some kind of instructor and she had heard of training accidents, and her son, Chick, didn't listen because he thought Joey was a bullying bastard, whose arrogance had been doubled by the Marine Corps, and her husband didn't listen because once the Korean war had ended, he spent no more time thinking about Joey, who was in the care of the U.S. government and off his list of responsibilities, but Mrs. Nester didn't need anyone to listen or respond, but needed only to unwind her spool of vague worry, while outside in the darkness that came suddenly now from the changing of the clocks stood the remnant of her son Billy, whose birth was an accident, four years after they had decided to stop having children, and whose death, as far as she knew, was also an accident, so that the life of Billy Nester was a slim volume held between bookends of chance on a high shelf that she noticed from time to time, but didn't pull down and leaf through.

Billy was close to the glass of the back door, closer than he had been to his family in a long while. He had been persuaded by Andy to try and be seen or felt by them because maybe that was the key, and Billy didn't believe in the key or even in the lock that Andy called "their purpose," and he supposed the only purpose was the waiting itself, which was no purpose at all, and he didn't like it, but he had never been able to influence his life by his likes or dislikes and so he accepted the same situation in his death.

He was there, outside the kitchen storm door, looking at the family that had been his family, not because he wanted to be there, but because he loved Andy and Emily who were his family now, and he was making this visit because tonight Andy and Emily were visiting their homes, too, and all this because of Myrna Gresha and what she had said to Andy, and because of what Billy had told them, because of the way his mother had wept once when he was near her and his brother had broken the car window, but now, looking through the doubled window, Billy was paid no attention, and yet he stayed, remembering all those hundreds of meals at this table where his brothers and father were silent and his mother talked and talked and no one took any notice of the youngest Nester when he had something to say about what had happened at school or what he had seen in the yard or the fields or what he had dreamed the night before, and many times he made up dreams he had never dreamed at all in order to capture their attention, but only his mother would give him a half-empty glance and then there would be nothing but the scraping and cutting and in summer the June bugs thumping the screen, but tonight it was too cold for bugs, and only Billy was at the screen door, and he stayed, even after he wanted to go away as far as he could. He stayed and no one noticed.

— · —

In the home of the Bridgers, Emily's mother was walking from the kitchen to the living room and back again, bringing dinner to the coffee table for herself and to the TV tray in front of his chair for her husband. He asked her to change the channel on the television, and she did, and he asked her to try the next channel, and she did, and he said turn it off, and she did, and then she went into the kitchen for his beer and her ginger ale and brought them and set them down and prepared to eat, and that's when he said, "So, you're never going to look at me?"

She stopped with her loaded fork in the air, but she didn't look at him. She put her food into her mouth and chewed, and she took a sip of ginger ale and said, "I look at you," without looking at him.

"You do not."

She turned to him then. "I'm looking at you now."

"Because I mentioned it."

She shrugged and went back to her meal. "I know what you look like."

"What do I look like?"

"Like Herb. Like my husband. Like her father. Her father. Her father. Her father." She drew out the word "father" in a mocking tone.

"What do you mean!"

"Her father. Her father. Her father."

"What are you saying?"

"You know what I'm saying."

"Then say it!"

"She's dead because of you."

"I loved her! I loved her more than you did! I never hurt her! The steering went out and she crashed! The steering!" He was crying as he shouted, the words moist and rough, and his wife, without looking at him, said, "That tree was supposed to be you. She crashed into you."

"She loved me!" His eyes were blurred and his mouth twisted. "She loved me, and I never hurt her."

"Liar. Liar. Liar. Liar. Liar. Liar."

He was sobbing in his chair. She looked at the wall, at the fake fireplace, at the dead television, and she said, "Liar. Liar. Liar. I know what you did. I know. I knew, I knew and I let. I let. I let. I let. I let. I let." And then she was silent, and, as her husband sobbed, she rose and left the house without a coat.

The remnant of her daughter, Emily, was standing on the front lawn, watching through the windows, standing as close to the house as she could because Andy had asked her to watch her parents and try to be noticed because maybe that was a

clue, maybe that would lead them to the reason for the waiting, maybe the contact was the important thing, but Emily saw
only the dim, lamplit figures of her parents eating a meal in
the living room, just the back of her father's head and the thin
form of her mother, serving a meal and eating and talking, and
then rising and…

When her mother came briskly out the door, Emily cried
out, seeing her so close to her. She could have touched her if
she could touch anything, but her mother didn't notice, moving quickly to the garage, her body tightened against the chill.
She pulled up the garage door and walked in and turned on
the light, and Emily followed her and stood just beyond the
open door and watched, fascinated just to see her moving and
bending and searching and reaching and living a life without
her daughter, living in a world that was minus Emily, and it
made Emily feel that she, herself, was nothing and nowhere,
and she couldn't stand to watch anymore, and she apologized
in her mind to Andy, and she left.

Emily's mother had not noticed the presence of her daughter's remnant. She was intent on her search and then, suddenly,
darted into a ragged pile of forgotten objects and clutched the
sign that had stood in the yard ten years ago when they tried
to sell the house and then changed their mind: FOR SALE. She
pulled it out of the pile by its long stake, receiving a sliver and
accepting the pain.

— · —

IN the home of the Cottermans, the family settled into "Drag-
net" on television and when it ended they separated as Andy's

mother sat at the kitchen table to plan the Thanksgiving dinner that she was forcing herself to make this year, writing out the shopping list, and Andy's sister studied for nursing school in her room, and Andy's dad watched two-thirds of a movie and fell asleep, and all the while the remnant of Andy stood in his old room and tried to move through the open door and enter the hall and come closer to his family, but he could not cross the doorway, and when he tried to force his way, he would be, suddenly, outside in the yard staring through the lighted windows.

So he waited in his room and looked again at everything on the walls and everything on the dresser and at the rug that had been on the floor forever that he did not remember ever studying before, and he studied its woven, faded colors and felt the house and the family settling into stillness around him.

He had no sense of the passage of time, but he looked at the progress of the clock on his old night table, and it was ten-thirty when his sister came into his room and turned on the light. He was thrilled by her proximity, holding his breath, though he had no breath, and feeling the increase of his heart, which wasn't there, and he watched her as she moved, so alive and so unaware of him, performing all the actions he would never perform again, turning on a lamp and turning off the wall switch to the overhead light, taking off a robe, sliding into a bed, standing up a pillow and pushing it into place and leaning back and opening a book and reading the pages.

He watched her read, watched her eyes move, and he felt not there. He felt not anywhere. He was in some kind of noplace, and he was waiting for nothing, and he didn't know why, and he couldn't figure it out.

He stood at the foot of his old bed and watched the sister he had loved through every stage of her life and whom he treasured, and he knew she treasured him, but she saw only her book and thought only her thoughts, and he felt that he might as well go, but he could not stop watching her, saying goodbye, he knew, with this final watching, and so he stood there and saw her eyes tire and close and open again, and he watched as she put down the book and rearranged the pillow and turned out the light, and then, although he had seldom been able to hear the living with any volume or clarity, he heard, or felt, her scream. It was not high-pitched, but low, like a shouted moan, and it had the weight of pain in it, and it shook and rippled the air like a blanket unfurled and snapped, and the air struck him like a wave, and then the lamp came on, but it was on its side. She had knocked it over and then found its switch, and she was holding the lamp, sitting up in bed, staring at him and crying out again in that same low, wrenching moan as his parents rushed into the room and Andy retreated to the corner, but his sister still stared at where he had been, and she pointed, and Andy could not hear the words clearly, but he knew she said, "Andy was there! He was right there!"

He saw his parents trying to comfort his sister, saw the anguish on her face and how she was shaking and saw the wetness at her eyes and under her nose as she sobbed and kept staring, staring at where her dead brother had stood, and he could not bear the anguish and the pain he had brought his sister and he made himself leave, and he was suddenly sitting in the frozen weeds of the ditch beside the highway where he had died.

If he had stayed, if he had lingered one more moment in his old room, he would have seen the tableau of his parents comforting his sister as they surrounded her on the bed, and seen his sister cover her face for a while, under the stroking of her parents' hands and voices, and then drop her hands to her lap and swallow until she could speak again, and he might have heard her or read her lips.

"Saying goodbye," she said. "He was saying goodbye."

And her parents continued the tender application of hands and words, saying, each in turn, "It was a dream, honey. It was a dream," and after a moment the daughter began to nod and to say, "Yes. Yes," her agreement easing her parents and satisfying them and leaving them out of the circle of her knowing, her absolute knowing.

—·—

ANDY sat beside the road for a long time and raised his head to the clear night sky and the disordered clusters of stars above him and felt a terrible longing. He could not feel the hard ground beneath him and he had no connection with the ice-bound space overhead, but he could not close his eyes because then he would see his sister's brutal shock and the sorrow of her torn heart, and he wanted so deeply, so terribly to hold her and even rock her in his arms.

Emily Bridger came to him then, and he was glad that he could look at her to keep his eyes from the blind sky and from his thoughts. "My mother didn't know I was there," Emily said, and Andy said, "Lie down with me."

They stretched out on the brittle, frosted vegetation and faced each other, just inches away, and imagined touching each other, and he was comforted by the illusion of her touch and the feel of her lips as they might have felt.

She asked, after a while, "What happened to you?"

But Andy only whispered, "Let's just stay like this, okay?" They stayed almost through to the dawn and then Emily rose up slowly on an elbow as if struck by a thought, and her stare was no longer given to him in full, but occupied with some mystery, and he asked her, "What?"

"Something's going on," she said, and she sat up, and as she moved, Andy's eyes widened and his mouth fell open because he could see a faint double image of her, her body rising to sit, and the transparent image of her still lying down and then following her body like a double exposure. He jolted to his knees, staring.

"Stand up," he said, and she stood, and he watched the image follow her and saw how the very edge of her, the line of her sweater, of her neck, her hair, was a blurred line. "Emily," he said.

"What's happening, Andy?"

"I think you're…"

They were suddenly at Emily's place then, at her tree, but it was changed. There were two cars parked off the highway, and one of them was a police car, it's top light revolving. At the tree were three men, including the lanky young officer that Andy knew, Ed Fontaine, and they were all staring at the tree, but not at the tree itself, at a sign that was propped against the tree. It leaned against the scarred birch on its long stake. It was a turned-around FOR SALE sign, and its blank back had been painted with a message, with careful blue letters on the wood, and the message read:

EMILY, I'M SORRY YOUR FATHER MOLESTED YOU, AND I'M SORRY I WAS AFRAID TO BELIEVE IT AND NEVER STOPPED IT. I'M SO SORRY. YOUR MOTHER. LOIS BRIDGER.

They all stared at the sign, the living and the remnants of the dead, and Emily felt herself weaken, and Andy came close to her, and the living men spoke to each other, but couldn't be heard by the dead, and in a while Billy Nester came, and he saw the sign and stood beside Emily and stared with wide eyes at her face and then at the blurring edges of her.

She was able to say "Look at that," to Billy, to Andy and to herself, say it dreamily, with wonder as she pointed to the sign. There it was, the sickness, there to be seen, to be heard, shouted, her mother's epistle to the world, her own truth glaring in the passing headlights, growing dim and then bright again, and Emily was surprised that she felt no pain, no horror, no shame, and she searched for words that described her feeling and found one and tasted it on her tongue. She felt, for once, unbroken. Her mother was saying *"Look!"* to everybody, to the whole town and to Emily, too, saying, *"Look, this happened,"* saying, "This is *true*," and saying, *"I'm sorry. I'm sorry."*

Emily's mother had come in the night with a flashlight and a hammer and her painted sign. She had tried to drive the stake into the dirt with the hammer, but the frozen ground would not accept it, so she had leaned the sign against the tree and then waited, standing beside the highway, but the first driver who passed only glanced at her and didn't see the sign, so she stepped out onto the pavement and waved the next driver to a stop. She said she had something to show him, and she walked him to the tree and showed him the sign and said, "Now you read that, and you call the police about it, and leave it there. You leave it there," and she drove away, and when she reached her home, she found that she was not sure the driver would do as she asked, so she called the police herself and told them about the sign and told them to leave it. Leave it there.

All through the dawn and into the morning, people came and went away, parking at the edge of the highway and reading the sign, and some took photographs of it, and seated nearby, in the woods, on the ground, were Emily, Andy and Billy, in a place where they could see the tree and the people, but, mostly, Andy and the boy watched Emily slowly change and fade. They seldom spoke, noting her progress as she felt herself disappearing, all of them awed by this slow, second dying, and, in time, Emily turned to them and smiled a small and loving smile, and she told them, "It's all right."

"Is it?" Billy asked her, and she nodded, and they saw the double image of her moving head, and saw how all of her was less than solid now and letting through the midday light. "Wonder where you'll go?" the boy said, his voice breaking.

Emily smiled again and raised her eyebrows and her shoulders in a slight and fading shrug, and her smile had some sadness in it, but the wonder was there, too, and a quiet but profound excitement, and Andy said, "Goodbye," while he still had her eyes, and she stared deeply at him, but could only nod, and then, soon, she wasn't seeing them anymore. They could tell. She was like Mrs. Groff and the others who came and left without seeing or knowing, but they stayed and watched her until the last impression of her was gone and there was just the daylight where she had been.

— · —

ANDY studied the emptiness that had been Emily and studied his thoughts, and it was much later when he spoke to the boy. His voice was deep and certain and was weighed down by a feeling that was leaden in his heart or what would have been his heart. He said the boy's name, and then he asked, "Do you want to go?"

Billy turned to him, shocked. "Me?"

"Do you want to go, Billy, if you can go?"

"You know how?!"

Andy nodded slowly and said, "I think so. Yeah, I think I do." And the boy stared in wonder and fear, too.

"So, you...know what we're supposed to do?"

Andy stood up and sighed heavily and looked again at the tree. There were no people there now, and the sign had been taken away. He said, "It's not what we're supposed to do, Billy. It's what *they're* supposed to do."

"Who?"

"The people who made us die," Andy said, and then he asked again, "Do you want to go? Do you want to finish this, all this waiting?" and the boy stared at him, studying this possibility with sharp intent.

"Will we be together? Where we're goin'?"

"I don't know, Billy."

"But maybe we will."

"Could be."

"Maybe she's waitin' for us."

"That's right," Andy said. "She could be waiting."

"She said it was all right," Billy said. "She seemed happy," and Andy nodded, and the boy, after a long while, said, "Yeah." He said it quietly, afraid to want it too much, afraid now that he wanted it, it might not happen. "How? How do I…?"

"Go see your brother."

Billy took that in, studying the idea and staring at the tree. "My brother isn't going to make some goddamn sign about me."

"You can try. You can be around him and try to make him notice you and remember, remember what he did, think hard about it. You can do that."

"He won't care," Billy said, and Andy let his anger loose then, shouting.

"For God's sake, Billy, you have a chance! At least you have a goddamn chance!"

Billy heard what wasn't said. He heard the part about Andy having no chance, because nobody caused his death, nobody around here, nobody he knew, and he understood why Andy was so mad, and sad, and he said, "Okay, Andy. Okay, I'll try, but…" He was afraid to finish, to say, "But what about you?" because there was no answer, so he began to move, and Andy moved with him, and then they were at Kosloski's gas station where Billy's brother worked.

They watched Chick Nester fill a car with gas and check the oil and clean the windows, talking all that time with the woman who was driving the car, and then they watched him step into the station and fix a flat tire and later clean his hands and comb his hair, and then he seemed to be swearing because two more cars were entering the station, and he was the only one there, and he went outside again, and Andy said to Billy that he should move closer to his brother and stay with him, stay very close, and this was difficult for Billy.

"He won't even know I'm there."

"He might," Andy said.

"It won't do any good," the boy said.

Andy was angry again. "Try it! Try it every goddamn day for a year, Billy. Jesus, what's the alternative? Fegg? Forty years? A hundred? Go on!"

— . —

CHICK Nester was angry because he never got to see anything. Every driver who came into the station was talking about the sign that Lois Bridger had put up where her daughter had died months ago, and he was sure they were going to take it away, the police would take it, and he'd never see it, and he never got to see the wreck, either, Emily's wreck at that tree, because Joe Kosloski did all the towing and didn't trust Chick to do it, even though Chick had watched him and knew how, and he had seen Emily Bridger's smashed car when it was towed in, but he didn't get to see it where he wanted to see it, smashed up against the tree, and he didn't get to see the Andy Cotterman wreck, either, two fatal wrecks just a couple of months apart, and he hadn't seen a thing, and now he was missing seeing the sign the mother had left, and he thought about the sign then and about Emily being molested by her father, and he had two thoughts. He wondered how any father could be so mean and so sick, and he thought about Emily Bridger naked and imagined being in bed with her, but he forced that thought away because she was dead and it was morbid, and he went back to being mad at his boss because Kosloski didn't trust him to take the tow truck, and then another driver came in and talked about the goddamn sign and told him it was gone now and speculated on the possibility that Emily had killed herself because of what her father had done, and said they should take Aaron Bridger out and shoot him for doing it with his own daughter, and Chick agreed and he added that they should castrate a guy like that, and then he was alone, and he wandered into the station and cleaned his hands again and combed his hair and looked at the pinup calendars that were never taken down, even when their years had passed, and then he thought about his brother Billy, and he didn't know why.

Any thought about Billy reminded him of the day at the lake, and any thought about that day made his stomach grow tight and cold, as if a stomach could freeze, and he fought against the ice inside of him by getting mad, so that his anger would pummel Billy, pummel all the Billys that came to mind, Billys of every age from maybe one until eleven, all of them being some kind of trouble or some kind of pest, and he would always end up swearing at Billy in his mind, asking why the hell Billy didn't just dogpaddle back to the pier, the jerk, the little jerk, and then...

The other thoughts came again, the old thoughts, marching again through his mind, the way he and his brother Joey both stopped laughing at the same second because Billy didn't come up and how they both jumped in and dived down and swam around looking, and how Chick's chest almost caved in, and he had to go up for air, knowing that when he came up for air he'd see Joey swimming and holding on to Billy and Billy would be all right, and Joey would be swearing at him, but when he came up for air, it was only Joey looking at him, and it was the worst look he ever saw, and then they both dived down again and again and found Billy, but it was too late.

Chick lost both his brothers that day, because Billy was dead and Joey was so afraid that Chick would tell about throwing Billy into the lake that Joey beat him. He beat him that day, and many times after that. When they were alone, Joey would shove him or wrestle him to the ground or slap the back of his head so hard it hurt his neck, just to remind him never, ever to tell, and Chick would never have told anyway, but Joey didn't believe him.

Another driver came into the station, but even as Chick serviced the car, he thought about Billy and the lake, and it made him more angry, because it was all Billy's fault, all the trouble was Billy's fault, even the trouble between Chick and Joey now, it was all because Billy would never leave them alone and always had to be with them, and he was still with them, the little jerk, the goddamn little jerk, and Chick worked faster on the cars and worked at pushing away his thoughts with anger and trying to twist them toward other things, toward the women in the pin-ups, toward the Saturday night movie at the drive-in with Laurentina Aguilar, toward the car he was rebuilding, and then Joe Kosloski came back to the station, and Chick was able to get away, and he went to see the tree, even though the police had taken the sign away.

— · —

THE remnant of his brother Billy was sitting high up on the inclining bank of the lake beside the remnant of Andy Cotterman, and the boy had his thin arms wrapped around his knees, with his head down on his kneecaps, and he wouldn't talk to Andy, but Andy kept trying. "Why does it feel so bad to be around him? Isn't it just as bad to be always in the woods, mostly alone?"

Billy didn't answer but shook his head, "No," by rocking it on his kneecaps.

"You have to get used to it," Andy said. "You have to do it every day." Billy shook his head again. "Why not?" Andy asked, and this time Billy spoke, still not lifting his head.

"Just reminds me. Reminds me too much."

"It's still worth it, Billy. It's still…"

It was quiet then, but there was something about Andy's broken word that made the boy lift his head from his knees and look at Andy, who was looking past him now, and Billy followed the look and saw his brother, Chick, coming out of the trees and walking along the edge of the water and stopping. They watched Chick study the lake, which was chopped by the wind today, and then turn his head to study the old pier. Andy and Billy said nothing and even imagined they were holding their breath, and they waited, and Chick started to move again, walking all the way to the pier and then out on the pier and staring into the water for a long time, and then moving to sit on the edge of the pier. He sat there for what might have been minutes or hours.

Billy and Andy had no gauge for the time and didn't check the sun's passage, didn't look away from Chick at all, Billy whispering once, "What's he supposed to do?"

"I don't know," Andy said, shaking his head slowly, "Maybe…" But that's all he said, and they continued watching until Chick stood up and walked away, moving out of sight into the trees, making his way back to the road and his car.

"He's not gonna do anything," Billy said, but Andy was watching him very carefully.

"What?" Billy said, and Andy said, "It's starting."

Billy jumped to his feet, looking at himself, and then at Andy, his face asking Andy and Andy nodding, but Billy couldn't see the fading. He moved his arm, and didn't see any change, and said to Andy, "Do you see it?" and this time, when Andy nodded, he was smiling a little, with some sadness, and Billy opened his mouth and drew in what would have been a deep breath and said, "I feel it now! Jesus Christ, Andy. God. Andy. God." And then he stared long at Andy, and he was shaking, and he said, "So, I'm going. God. I'm really going…like Emily, and…all of them, and I wonder…what will it be? And… Jesus, Andy, Jesus, you'll be alone…except for Fegg."

In a while, Andy said, "Somebody might come," and Billy nodded and then spoke more quickly, shaking more violently. "I want to say goodbye, Andy. I want to say goodbye before I… And I want to say goodbye to Fegg, too. I hate 'im, but I want to say goodbye."

"I'll tell him," Andy said, keeping his sad smile and watching the boy begin to thin, as a cloud thins, the sun slowly erasing it from the sky. The last of Billy nodded at Andy, and Andy nodded to the disappearing boy.

When it was over, Andy walked to the lumber yard, making sure he took every step and did not spring ahead. He wanted to feel as if he was actually walking, and he wanted to spend the time generously because he had so much of it, but when he reached the yard and saw the old man on the roof, the mean old man whose killer had never been sorry, he didn't want to talk to him. He didn't want to be near him, and he didn't want to give him Billy's name and Billy's goodbye, so that the bitter old fool could curse the boy. He would tell Fegg some other time, some other year, because Billy wanted him to, but he would not tell him today.

That night Andy was at his place beside the highway, and in the morning, he was still there, sitting in the ditch, his hands in his jacket pockets and elbows winged out. He waited, thinking of the man who had killed him, the driver of the truck who had, for some reason, come into his lane. Maybe the man wanted to die or to hurt somebody, or maybe he fell asleep or he was drunk or he just drifted and didn't notice until it was too late, and all Andy knew of this man is that he was a driver of trucks, but maybe he was the kind of man who would confess his killing and his sorrow to a priest, or to a minister or to a wife or to a friend at a bar as he shed tears in a drunken, mournful, spilling of grief.

Andy watched the highway then, thinking that if this man was still driving trucks, then he just might drive again along this highway, and if he did, and if he passed this spot, and if Andy were here to help remind him, it's just possible that the man might send, if not a prayer, at least a thought, at least one brief thought of atonement.

The Painter Loon

THERE WAS A TIME IN THE 1950's when everyone in Indian Lake, Illinois, knew just what goods and services were offered there and where they were offered and who was offering them, and this was because of the signage. These were hand-painted wooden signs of all sizes and also lettering on windows and glass doors and on the shingles of the two dentists and the doctor and the attorney who served this town, one of a chain of villages gathered beside the placid lakes of the northern prairies, protected by fifty miles of forest and agriculture from the hungry reach of the Chicago suburbs.

The signs were precise and even beautiful, and they were all the work of F. Van Loon, a refugee from Chicago's great welter of voices who came to Indian Lake hungry for solitude and seclusion.

He was fifty-five then, a tall, strong, bulky man, slow-moving and dark in every sense, his skin tanned, hair and beard black and raggedly self-cut, eyes like soft coal reflecting an antique pain, and a weighty face often still and somber. He walked with a slight limp, the shadow of an old accident, and the uneven tread made the ponderous man appear more ponderous, but when he held a brush, and when he brought that brush to the surface of a sign, the man became delicate and certain and deft and exact.

Only one of these signs still exists today, attached to a building that used to house the Tip Top Grocery. The faded board still names the ghost of that store in broad red letters weathered now to a tired pink, every letter perfectly straight and expertly spaced, but beyond the precision, there is beauty in the intricate checkerboard border of red, blue and yellow and in the figures decorating each corner of the sign, which have no connection with the store it named or the products it sold.

Van Loon used to put fanciful boats in the corners, a toymaker's idea of a Dutch boat, or he would create whimsical airplanes or animals, tiny dancers, whatever was hiding in his brush that day, but this one remaining sign is from the time when he was painting only roses in the corners, fully bloomed reds on gracefully curving stems, each flower seven inches tall and still visible from the street, still visible today, and it was during this time, the time of Van Loon's roses, that his neighbors and the town council and finally the Indian Lake Police began to think that Van Loon might be insane and wondered if he should be put away for his safety and their own.

He came to town in 1954 and purchased a small building

with store space fronting the highway and living quarters above, and even before he moved in, he painted his first Indian Lake sign, stretching eight feet across the building front and three feet high. VAN LOON, it said modestly, but then it shouted, SIGN PAINTER, showing courage in the choice of a different color for each letter, revealing imagination in its border of triangles in soft blue, like a distant and endless range of mountains, and smiling in its corners where four cartoon boats sailed on wisps of a green and foamy sea.

His possessions were not many but seemed carefully chosen, and the people of the town, passing in their vehicles or walking by on their way to the lake or to the small town center, watched him carry into his new home both antique furniture and furniture made by his own hand and painted by his brush. There was a great clock, held carefully in his embrace like a taller brother, and two paintings that stretched his arms to their limit, one depicting a Dutch harbor and the other showing a woman, nude, kneeling in a shallow pond that was engulfed by jungle greenery, a large bird of explosive colors just now springing from a branch and taking with it the glance of the nude beauty and her smile.

A young contractor, Carl Fanucci, stopped his truck in the middle of the highway to watch the passage of this painting in the spreading arms of the sign painter and was captured by the smiling young woman who was rocking through the air to the off-beat of Van Loon's limping step. Fanucci held his breath as Van Loon edged carefully through his doorway, the contractor's mouth slightly open as he followed the wet, shining body and the face of the girl until she was taken into Van Loon's dark home like a hostage. Then Fanucci brought his truck into motion again and drove home quickly to his wife, Paula, led her to the sofa and impregnated her with their second child.

That same evening, Fanucci returned to Van Loon's shop and saw on the closed door a painted sign with no words, but with an image that spoke clearly. It was the picture of a closed padlock, a full twenty inches tall and startlingly blue against an orange background. There could be no misunderstanding this sign, and Fanucci hesitated. He could hear sounds within, and there were lights in the windows of the second floor, so the contractor, full of his mission, raised a fist and knocked.

Upstairs, arranging his furniture, Van Loon paused and disappointment settled on him like a heavy coat. Someone had come, and now he would have to speak. Someone had ignored his sign, and now discourse would be forced upon him. He swallowed and sighed and lumbered down the staircase into his shop, turned on the light and opened the door, which had not been locked, except by the sign.

"Yess?" Van Loon spoke softly in English that was not broken, but, after seventeen years in America, still accented with a kind of filigree of European sounds.

"Hi, I'm Fanucci, Carl Fanucci."

"Mm."

"You're a sign painter, right?"

This Van Loon would not answer. He spoke fewer words each month, using them like the last bullets of a man surrounded.

"I'd like you to paint a sign for my truck, a wooden sign that I'll put up on the side rails, but I want two, one for the left side and one for the right, so people can read it if I'm comin' or goin', if I'm parked on the left of the street or the right, see?"

"Mm."

"I got it written out here: 'Fanucci Building and Repair' and then I got the phone number." He handed a sheet of paper to Van Loon, the words carefully printed in pencil along with ruler lines and dimensions. Van Loon studied the instructions, swelled his large chest and then collapsed it with an epic sigh. He looked at the contractor, his bearded jaw rolling slightly as if some heavy and rusty machinery was being set into motion.

"Da people here...dey know you and...wat you do?"

"Sure. They know me. I grew up here."

"Eight days," Van Loon said.

"You'll do it?"

This he also refused to answer, but since the contractor was waiting, he offered another nod.

"How much?"

"*You* will say."

"I will say? The price?"

Van Loon gave one more nod, closing his eyes to finalize the conversation.

"Well...okay. Eight days then." Fanucci reached out his hand and left it suspended there while the sign painter looked at it, made a judgment, took the hand and gave it a gentle shake. When they dropped hands, Fanucci continued to stare, revealing just the skin of a deep longing.

"You got a painting. I guess…somebody saw it when you moved in today. They said it's a real good painting. Of a woman. And a…bird. Some kind of jungle bird."

Van Loon was forced to give one more nod.

"I'd sure like to get a look at that…bird."

The big man stared with eyes that held an old pain, and after a silence long enough to make Fanucci jumpy, he turned away and began to march up the stairway to his living quarters like a man mounting the gallows. The younger man wasn't certain if he should follow, but waited hopefully, and when Van Loon half turned, Fanucci marched behind him.

The sign painter was asking himself why he was allowing this intrusion into his private life and private rooms and decided it was pride and wondered why he hadn't erased that word from his mind as he had erased so many others. They walked to a windowless wall where both the paintings hung, and they halted, shoulder to shoulder. Fanucci swallowed audibly, eyes moving slowly over the wet nude girl as if he were gently toweling her and then returning to the smile that lit her face and to her eyes. He said, "Wow" or "God" or some other barely voiced word, and Van Loon said, with his old and quiet pride, "My sister."

"She's your sister!?"

"Da painter," the older man said, his stare moving like a slow pendulum, studying fondly the Dutch harbor, the jungle scene, and back again, the oils Greta had given to him as they parted. There had been too many partings, and now there could be no more.

"And what's the name of…?" Fanucci's hand moved over the jungle scene like a benediction.

Van Loon said, "Macaw."

"Her first name," Fanucci asked.

"Da bird," said Van Loon. "Macaw. Da girl… I don' know. A model."

"Oh." Fanucci was disappointed but relieved, too, to find that he would not, after all, be spending his life tracking this woman through the jungles of the world. Nothing was said for minutes, then the contractor spoke. "Thanks for showing me. I'll…see you then. Eight days."

When Van Loon heard Fanucci leaving through his front door, he picked up a chair and moved it to face the wall of paintings. He sat, and for a man so thrifty with words, was generous with sighs, looking through the oils to the memories: Greta leaving on the train with her soldier, Greta writing him from California, inviting him to come.

He had sent her a picture of himself waving to her, not waving hello, but goodbye, and he drew his face smiling so she would know he wished her well and still loved her, but he would not be visiting her. He could not move through a million people and a hundred conversations to arrive at her home with his weight of sorrows like a traveler's heavy trunk.

He was the family's keeper of sorrows, and he collected them in a sketch book. There was the girl-who-broke-his-heart. This was in Holland, long ago, and he had tried to draw her face, but human faces are imprecise, and he rendered only an impression of her. For his mother, taken so swiftly by disease, he would not degrade her likeness, so he drew the hospital, the architecture of her pain. For his father, who a year later took his own life, he drew an empty bridge. He had brought his sister and young brother to America then, just as the kindling of Europe was catching fire, and he painted signs and also painted ships in the navy yard and paid for art lessons for his sister and school for his brother, Peter, but the young man was restless and enlisted in the army and was consumed by the fire, and when Van Loon tried to draw an image to signify this calamity, he found that his hand drew only a circle, and he studied this and realized it was a picture of emptiness.

— . —

IN eight days Fanucci returned, seeing that the door to Van Loon's shop was closed and bearing a different painted sign, a large padlock again, bright blue on bright orange, but this padlock was painted open. He entered and saw that his signs were ready. They were displayed on the walls in the exact dimensions he had ordered, in vivid colors that caught and held and pleased the eye, but the words were not what he had asked for. There was only one word on each sign: his name, FANUCCI, large and brave and singing there, in multicolored letters. After the name came the images of three houses, pretty houses, like trophies, pictures that defined perfectly what Carl Fanucci offered to the people of the lake towns. Beneath the happy homes, which had chimneys and even wisps of smoke, were the numbers of Fanucci's phone. The contractor stared at the signs, stared at the precision and the beauty and the joy, and arranged a generous offer of payment in his mind.

Van Loon helped Fanucci mount the signs on his truck, received his payment, and then consented to another visit between Fanucci and the jungle girl. He only pointed to his staircase and let the younger man ascend to his rooms and stare at Greta's fanciful scene, while he went back to work on the sign for BARBARA'S BEAUTY SALON — HAIR AND NAILS, which came out of his brush without the words HAIR AND NAILS, but with coiffed heads in two of its corners and graceful hands in the others, each fingernail a bright scarlet, and with an unasked-for border of tiny cupids at the top, but before he finished the cupids, Joe Kosloski of KOSLOSKI'S GAS AND TOWING also came to his shop and ordered a new sign, but received it a week later with only the word KOSLOSKI'S on it and a picture of an animated tow truck and a bulbous, smiling gas pump. Van Loon had drawn comic books for his younger brother, and he knew how to make a gas pump smile. Kosloski asked politely if Van Loon was sure that people would "get it."

Van Loon asked him in return, "Da sign — it will be at your gas station, no?" and Kosloski stared and then slowly grinned.

The rich harvest of work brought problems to Van Loon, who was more in retreat than ever, yet people visited, unafraid of knocking on his door, padlock or not, Kosloski coming in the evening to inquire if Van Loon was a bowler, and if he might want to join his team, and Fanucci bringing cold beers one night to gain another audience with the nude jungle beauty who would not leave his mind, while Barbara of the beauty salon, misinterpreting the cupids on her sign, asked Van Loon over for an awkward dinner. She offered to wash and cut his hair that very night after dessert, but because she kept the air so dense with words and finished every one of his sentences, guessing at what he intended to say, he excused himself with gracious thanks and left.

The people were not drawn to him by his shaggy, hulking appearance or by his meager conversation, but by the Van Loon they saw revealed in his signs, by the imagination and the humor and the wisdom and the feast of color they knew must live somewhere inside the sign painter, and they came to gather around the inner Van Loon as if around a small, banked fire. Uncomfortable with the foreign structure of his name, they shortened it to "Loon," and used it as a first name, as a friendly offering like a hand held out, and they waited for Loon to take the hand. He was a man who did not wish to be rude, but did not wish to communicate beyond his brush, and this led to a decision that would begin Van Loon's slide, in the minds of the people of the lake towns, from eccentricity to possible insanity.

He kept his shop on the highway, but moved his home to the most remote property for sale in all of Indian Lake, the old Cass place that had not been lived in for six years. It offered two overgrown acres and was far enough off a bad road to be invisible and discouraging to visitors. He moved in quickly, foregoing the needed repairs in order to be away. He assembled his furniture and sat in the silence of the rooms as if in a warm bath, and he closed his eyes. There were mice in the walls, but they did not ask for any words. A tilted porch, walled by a torn screen, could be a work space so that he might go to his shop only two days a week to receive more customers, to deliver his signs, to communicate what was necessary, and the rest of his days could be deserted and mute.

He hung his paintings. He fixed the kitchen stove. He tramped through his forested and brush-tangled property. There was a rusty hand pump that brought water from the well, cool and metallic on his tongue. There was an old foundation that tripped him and sprawled him on the dirt floor of what had been a cabin, the walls and roof gone long ago. He stood and followed the outline of the stones and rotted timbers. It had been a small cabin, ten by twenty. He uncovered the hearthstone and remembered the disinterested agent telling him the property had been settled "way back before the Civil War." He stood in the ghost of the old cabin and looked all about and saw nothing but trees and weeds and the thick wild berry bushes. Even his house was out of sight and even the shed and the old pump. Only the natural world surrounded the cabin site, and he wondered if the dweller here had been a man like him who was moving toward solitude like an arrow, a man who shed words like dead skin, another Van Loon.

He stepped out of the cabin site and caught a movement at the corner of his vision and turned and saw nothing. The image had been pale and fleeting, someone's skin showing through the trees, part of a face, someone watching him, an intruder? He waited and listened, not afraid but feeling assailed and annoyed. He would construct a fence if he needed to, a tall fence.

In the warm-blooded darkness of a country summer night, as he teetered over the pit of sleep, he heard a sound muffled by the cotton of his semi-consciousness. It could have been the rusty whine of the old pump. But who would be at his pump? And just one stroke? He didn't rise into wakefulness, but in the morning he remembered.

He could not straighten the floor of the porch himself, and the roof needed repairs that were beyond his skill. He would have to ask workers to come. He would have to talk to them. He put this off, but the damp, moldy smell of the bad wood annoyed him, and the mice enacted, over the first two nights, an industrial revolution in his walls. On the third night, heavy and humid, he took a drop-cloth and two blankets and looked for a place to sleep outdoors.

By flashlight he found the old cabin site and cleared the floor of sticks, stones and clumps of earth, and laid the drop-cloth down and one blanket. He sat and took off his boots, used his bundled jacket for a pillow and eased back to rest his head and saw above him the white dust of the universe, more clear, more vast than ever before, so that he opened his mouth slowly, in sudden acceptance of these worlds beyond, and it was then that he heard the sound again, the one still in his memory, the faint screech that could have been a stroke of the pump, but wasn't. It was a living sound, a sound made by throat and lungs and air. An animal? What makes such a sound?

He listened and heard only the rustle of wind in leaves, like the movement of a taffeta skirt, and his eyes grew small. When he turned on his side a woman stepped out of his memory, unbidden, a sad woman from the Chicago apartment house, the married woman upstairs who had come to him to spend, once a week, a guilty hour in his bed, listening, at times, to the tread of her husband across their ceiling. Her visits lasted nearly a year, and then came no more, and this was another loss, but he had not entered her in his book of losses, always knowing she would not last, and he missed only the wordless contact of flesh, sometimes smooth and pliant, sometimes stiff and trembling, the movement of bodies under a blanket, joining and parting and joining like elemental life, the fundamental dance that now escaped him, so that he stood apart even from the crickets and night birds and field mice that teemed around him, lying in the ghost of a cabin, out of reach.

In his dream, the woman came to him, the woman in Chicago who always whispered, dark hair, dark eyes full of fear and longing, and she touched his face very lightly, so tenderly that he had to swallow tears, and then another hand, a small hand, smaller than the hand of the woman in Chicago, was stroking his heavy beard and then, suddenly, pulling it, yanking it hard at his cheek, and he awoke crying out, because this was so very real. He felt the residue of pain on his face, and he found himself up on an elbow, blinking into the darkness, his breathing heavy, his heart a drum. He noticed that he had an erection, but before he could examine this surprising gift, he heard a scrape on the ground behind him, the scrape a foot might make on the earth, a bare foot, and he turned quickly.

He saw legs, a woman's legs moving in the pale starlight, white and bare in the starlight, and they ran, in just two bounds, toward the deeper darkness of the trees and bushes and were gone, and above the legs there had been only the shadowy possibility of a body, but at the top there had been hair, following like a flag, streaming, shining, possibly golden but looking silver in the starlight and seen for only one bright sliver of a second.

He was standing now, the drum of his heart rushing its tempo. He took a step toward the enclosing foliage and paused to speak, but he had shed so many words, none came for a long while, and then he shouted, "Who?" like some giant bearded owl. "Who…are you?" The crickets stopped their rhythm, and the entire night listened, but only the wind came and rustled the skirts of the meager forest and the dense shrubs.

He stepped back to his blankets, and then sat on them, suddenly chilled and alone, accepting that he had been dreaming. He shoveled in a great breath and blew it out, accepting that his dream and the starlight had caused him to see what was not there, but then he stroked his face where his beard had been pulled. It was sore. And what about that length of streaming hair?

— · —

HE spent the next day at his shop on the highway, packing the last of his supplies, gathering more orders, all the while distracted and fingering, unconsciously, one side of his beard. He spoke to Fanucci and agreed on a date for the estimating of the repairs of his home, Carl to bring his brother, Johnny, a roofer, and then he was finished with all the discourse of business and could return to his sanctuary, the town visit having cost him eighteen words.

In the twilight, he inspected the cabin site, smoothed the ground, added a tarp for the floor, looked above to judge the cloudless sky and slowly surveyed all the nearby foliage watching for what? For whom?

At the time of full darkness, he came outside with his flashlight, two blankets and a second tarp to keep off the dew. He was dressed in an undershirt and wide shorts and boots that were untied on his bare feet. He felt foolish, but told himself that he was only sleeping here because it was too warm and too moldy in that busy city of rodents he called his house.

Straining to listen, he could not sleep. He closed his eyes and tried to empty his mind, but found that his mind was now occupied with emptying. He blew out a frustrated breath, and that's when he heard her. This was not a pump or even an animal. This was clearly an outcry made by a woman's voice, a kind of whimper, a high note, plaintive. He opened his eyes and ceased all other motion, even his blood seemed to pause in its circular journey. He waited. There was no other sound, but there was something. He was lying on his side—and felt certain there was a presence behind him. He could not hear its breath or smell its scent. The air did not move, but he knew that someone was very near. He was afraid to turn around, not afraid of shock or pain or death, but afraid that there was no one there and that he was going mad. He wanted there to be someone lying behind him in the dark, not only to preserve his sanity, he realized suddenly, but because he simply wanted someone with him in the night, and this surprised him, this man driven toward solitude like an arrow. In this moment, Van

Loon uncovered a hunger beneath the floor of his consciousness, beyond his wish for reclusion. He found that he wanted
someone to be sharing his exile with him, wordlessly, a silent
somebody breathing beside him, since so many had gone away,
and so, finally, with a mad hope, he turned onto his back and
looked across his body and found that the air was empty, and
the ground was empty, and the night was empty except for the
insects and night birds and mammals of the inner earth and
Van Loon himself, and he felt his eyes submerge in a thin stra-
tum of tears.

His large chest heaved and collapsed like a great bellows,
and he made his own sound, surprising himself, a brief, liquid
moan, and then she answered it, the woman, the woman who
was not there, answered his small wet moan with another fragile
whimper in a high register, two voices, two seldom-used voices,
allowing their small and secret complaints to be heard by each
other, and by no one else.

He gasped and turned again to search the darkness, and
there was no one. He sat up and reached for his flashlight, but
now the presence was there again, just behind him, needles at
the back of his neck, and he twisted, and this time shouted at
the emptiness there, and there was anger and longing in the
wordless shout. He gripped his head and rested his elbows on
his knees and wept for himself, for Van Loon finally and fully
alone and now wanting another, for Van Loon suffering one
more loss, for Van loon going mad.

He dropped down on the blankets, curled on his side, fighting and winning the battle against his own weeping. He had

wept enough. All the tears had been wrung out of him. This
would be the last, then, this pitiful outburst of an aging man
alone on the dirt floor of an abandoned ruin, such an image
of sorrow that it made him laugh suddenly, a wretched laugh
that boomed inside of him and tore at the night, a laugh at his
own self-pity, mocking and forgiving himself in the same deep
guffawing, and when he was done, and the laughter trailed into
a few echoing chuckles, he moved to wipe his fingers over the
wetness beneath his eyes, and that's when he felt her lie down
beside him, pressing herself against his back.

He swallowed his laughter and his weeping and lay there.
"Oh my good Christ," he said in Dutch, in his mind. He could
not hear her breathing, but he could feel her against him, and
she was moving now, softly. "Dis is happening," he said in
English, in a reverent whisper, as one of her arms crept over his
side and around to his chest, riding the rise and fall of his own
careful breath. The weight of her arm, her hand, was not imagined, not imagined. He repeated this to himself many times.
"Dis is not imagined. I am awake." Very slowly, he moved his
fingers toward that hand, hesitating between madness and sanity, which would now be determined by the next movement of
his fingers, and he moved his fingers, and he touched her, and
she was there.

Her hand was chilled, and he covered it to bring warmth.
It was rough and dry, small in his palm, but not fragile. He
pressed it against his chest. She moved even closer behind him,
her knees pressing the backs of his legs, her head rubbing his
back in a settling, snuggling motion, and then she was still. He

swallowed. He tamed his breath so that it came evenly, calmly. She seemed relaxed along his back, her arm wrapping his bulk, her hand inside his, so that he settled, too, muscle by muscle, easing into the blankets and the tarps and the ancient earth, closing his eyes, keeping her small, strong hand pressed against the quiet, steady engine of his heart.

He allowed himself to close his eyes and even, in time, to ease the pressure on her hand. It remained against his chest without him clasping it there, as her knees remained against the backs of his thighs and her forehead burrowed into his back. He did not dare turn to look at her, and he did not dare speak. He willed himself to accept what was given. It was enough, for now, this tender proximity, this mute physical comforting. He wondered if she was as naked as her arm that lay across his ribs. The legs he had glimpsed the night before had been all pale skin. This thought sent an alarm to his loins and began the automatic readying of the machinery there, but he willed this activity to cease, and he only lay there, sending her whatever solace she received from his body-warmth and bulk.

Much later, as he slept, she came to him. He never saw her face. He felt her trying to turn him, and he turned, and she pressed her small, muscular body against him, and it was a nude body, and his arms encircled her, unsure, until she began to pull his undershirt upward, but found it trapped. She let go and grabbed into the sides of his beard to bring him close, and she kissed him fiercely, pulling with her fists in the hairs of his beard so that he cried out and then engulfed her mouth in his own and touched her everywhere, and she opened to him, and he awoke, and it was morning, and he was alone.

His heart was drumming, and he was chilled and naked, his undershirt and shorts strewn on his blankets. He looked for her. He looked for any sign of her. He cried out, bellowing something wordless, some guttural shout that spoke of desperate anger and the fear of madness that still lingered because she was gone, and what if she had never come to him, what if she didn't exist? He looked at his hand that had held her hand and remembered its physical imprint, its weight. He remembered her hair, thick and long and silver in the light, but probably golden, golden hair.

He grabbed at his strewn clothing and swept it up and stood, anger in his movements, but then he halted, because in standing he felt a crustiness on the skin of his thigh, and he touched it with his fingertips. He had spilled there. His sexuality had burst and spilled in the night, and so his anger evaporated then, leaving him feeling ashamed and pathetic, an aging man who had dreamed a woman into his bed and made himself wet with longing, nothing else, no more than that. He stepped into his dew-moistened boots and walked through the weeds and bushes to his house and through the back door, dropping his shorts on a table there, and on top of them his white undershirt, and then he paused and held still a long while, staring at his shirt, and then reaching toward it, slowly, carefully. There were three long hairs attached to the fabric on the back of his shirt, three blond hairs. He sat at the rough table, tweezing each hair with blunt finger and thumb and pulling it away, holding it up to the morning light that shined at the window. One of the hairs was at least two feet in length and golden; they were all golden.

He put them back on the shirt with great care and slowly folded the fabric to keep them safe, and he rose from the table and walked outside, walked to the cabin site and inspected the blankets and tarps. He found one more hair in the blankets and carried it pinched in finger and thumb as he studied the ground, but found no footprints among the weeds. He began walking through all his property, moving around the thickest bushes and trees, studying the ground and arriving at a mostly ruined rail fence. Across the fence was a patch of lawn and a neighboring house, and on the porch of that house stood a woman, staring at him, perhaps thirty yards away, staring at the ponderous bulk of this man who stood naked in his untied boots, his thick hand pinching carefully something invisible to her. The woman was heavy and seventy or so, and he shouted at her.

"You live der?"

"Who are you?! Go away!"

"I am Van Loon! I live here! You live der?!"

"Yes! With my husband! He's right inside! You better go away!"

"Only you?" he asked her, and her words became more and more shrill.

"What?!"

"Only you and your husband live der?!"

"We have a shotgun!"

"Only you two live der?!"

"Yes! We have a loaded shotgun! Go away now!" Her final words were half screamed, and he nodded and turned and walked away, and she watched him until he was out of sight, and then hurried into her house, past the room where her husband lived mostly in his bed, and she picked up the phone and broke into a call on her party line. "This is May, and you know what I just saw?!"

Van Loon washed himself and dressed and was eating bread and cheese, seated on his tilting porch, a signboard on the table in front of him, hoping that work would pull him away from the questions and answers that collided in his head like cymbals. Who is she? What is she? Is she? Yes. There's the hair. And the feel of her! A sheet of paper rested on the signboard, reading, DR. ROBERT SAUER, VETERINARY MEDICINE, LARGE AND SMALL ANIMALS. His client would receive only VETERINARIAN with a small DR. R. SAUER beneath that, but in each corner Van Loon would paint an exquisite animal, an animal with a life inside, with a soul, and he began sketching them now, dog, cat, horse, and what else? He smiled, a nearly hidden movement inside his heavy beard, at the inspiration to add the jungle bird from Greta's painting, and he froze his face in the rare aspect of smiling and limped to a mirror he had not yet unpacked, pulling it from its box and tearing off its protective paper and staring at himself, at Van Loon smiling the ordinary, contented and slightly dopey smile of a man who had begun his day making love to his woman, not just any man, but a wanderer for years across a sexual desert who had just found a lagoon.

He had this smile on his face when the trucks came, and then the voices. He didn't like hearing the words of others in his sanctuary, but they went on, two voices in quick conversation, too far for him to hear the words, and then there was a boom against his house and footfalls on his roof: the Fanuccis, inspecting the structure. He ignored them as he would ignore chattering birds and went back to the sketch for his sign, feeling inspired, without any reason that was clear to him, to add a border of tiny roses across the top, red blooming roses on curving stems. It was the first time he had used the roses, and he was sketching the flowers when the Fanucci brothers came down from the roof and entered his home with their heavy boots and their river of talk. He stopped his brush above the sign and sighed. Their sounds had now shaped into words, so many words loose in his home, like wasps.

"My heel just went through the floor. Hee hee hee. Right here, look."

"Yeah, this wall's a sponge, the whole wall. Just broke off a piece, like a cookie, look at this. Gingerbread house. Smell it."

"I don't want to smell it."

"Mold."

"No shit, Sherlock. Where *is* this guy. Loon?!"

"Oh, Johhny, Johnny, look. There she is. Look at the painting!"

"Who's she?"

"What'ya mean, 'who's she,' lead-head. She's a jungle girl. Don't you love her?"

"She's wet."

"I know. Isn't that great? She's wet all over 'cause she's been swimmin' in the pond and now she's just kneelin' there, smilin' at the bird. See that bird?"

"I'm still studyin' her tits."

"It's a macaw."

"Ever really *see* nipples that were so cherry red like that, bright red? You know who had tits like that? Remember Ellen Zane? Junior year? Like red cherry Lifesavers."

"Never saw 'em."

"Tasted like cherry Lifesavers, too. I swear to God."

"Bullshit, you never tasted 'em. Now, look. Look at her. Don't you wish you were standin' there in the jungle, and she doesn't see you yet, and you just found her like that, and you're watchin' her?"

"I'm already in the water with her, and you're still in the jungle. I've got a Lifesaver in my mouth."

"You're so full of shit."

"You just watch from the jungle while she and I splash around in that pond and then come out and catch that bird and have it for lunch."

"You're a butthole, y'know?"

"Where *is* this guy?"

"Here."

They turned toward the porch and saw him enter the living room, and Johnny Fanucci, who had never seen Van Loon, took a step back from the man's size and strangeness, but then talked on without interruption, his brother taking part in the rapid conversation like two boys playing catch.

"Wood up top is like cheese. You need a new roof, the whole shebang. I brought some shingles down to show ya. Swiss cheese."

"Foundation looks all right so far. Some of the floors are dry. Kitchen's dry. Look at these water stains, though. Smell the damp?"

Van Loon tried to guide them to the ending, toward the silence that would come back when they left.

"How long will dis take...to fix?"

"Three weeks on the roof if no storms come through. Tell me, buddy, would you sell that painting?"

"The painting! Wait a minute—I saw it first. I been looking at it for weeks now."

"Well, I like it, too. Gives me a taste for a Lifesaver. You wouldn't have any candy around here, would you, Mr. Loon?"

"I haff no candy."

"Uh-huh. Uh-huh. You a Heinie? You a German man?"

"I am Dutch."

"Uh-huh. When did you come over here from Dutchland?"

"From Holland, headcheese."

"I *meant* Holland."

"Knock it off, Johnny. The man says he's Dutch."

"Uh-huh. Uh-huh. They all say that though. You fight in the war?"

"I was too old."

"Uh-huh. Well, I seen pictures of Heinie officers old like you. Great uniforms. Right? Great uniforms. Put our own officers to shame. Me and my brother Carl were still in trainin' when you people surrendered, so we never got to go over, but we lost two cousins and an uncle with no legs now, not even one. So…three weeks, you get a brand-new roof. It'll last longer than you will. Guaranteed. So…you get homesick for Berlin?"

"The porch looks shot." Carl tried to lead them away, but Van Loon stepped closer to the jungle painting and stared at the girl, at her hair that was close against her head, wet and shining.

"What color? You say—her hair."

This surprised the brothers and halted their chatter. Then Johnny began again. "Kinda light. Reddish. You sellin' that painting?"

"He's not sellin' 'cause his sister painted it, lugnut, and it's auburn. Auburn hair."

Van Loon was nodding. "Der is a woman. Golden hair. Long. Da hair is long. Da woman iss…" He put out a flat hand, measuring the height of a woman shorter than the Fanuccis. "You know her? She is maybe…tirty. You see her? Near here?" He was tired from the sudden escape of so many words.

The Fanuccis looked at each other—and then did a common shrug. Van Loon moved away from the painting and led them to the porch, wondering if he was so different from Carl Fanucci, both of them captured by the image of a naked woman, but his own was a tangible woman. There was the hair. There was the palpable memory.

"This ain't a porch, Loon. It's a hill. You could sled on this porch."

"Wasn't made right." Carl pulled at a four-foot floorboard, its nails sliding out at one end with hardly a squeak. "Joists've rotted out. Used nails where there shoulda been screws. Not weather-tight out here, either. Sloppy job."

Johnny grabbed the same board and pulled it all the way out of the floor, held it up to show that it was bowed in spite of its one-inch thickness. "Look how warped," he said, "Kaput. That's what you say, ain't it? Kaput." And he tossed the board onto the table, missing the sign-in-progress, but landing with one end on the carefully folded white undershirt. Van Loon stared hotly at the mussed shirt and then limped toward it. He removed the board carefully from the fabric and spread the shirt. There were no hairs.

"Der were hairs." His voice shook. "Long gold hairs. Here!" He turned the shirt and spread it again. He looked closely at the tabletop. "Lost!" The Fanuccis stared at each other. "Da woman's hair. Lost now!"

"Sorry, Loon," Carl began, but his brother was streaming words again.

"What the hell are you talkin' about? If that's the woman's shirt, where's the woman, and what's she wearin' now? That's what I want to know, and what're you keepin' her hair for, anyway? You mean a lock of her hair? You mean the little blonde you were talkin' about? Hell, let's look around for her. She German, too?"

"Lost!" Van Loon boomed the word as he struck the board with a heavy, tightened fist, causing the table and the men to jump and splitting the floorboard neatly in half.

"Jesus Christ, Carl, he split the board. It's a one-by, and he split the damn board. Did you see me jump?"

"You're still jumpin'."

"I guess he's mad."

"I guess he's Dutch."

"Hey, I'm sorry, buddy. Take it easy. We'll help you look."

Van Loon grasped one end of the split board and lifted it from the table, his eyes burning Johnny Fanucci. "Lost," he said, a word he had used so often and was using again. Johnny took another step back.

"Hey, hey if you want to find something… Tell 'im, Carl. If you want to find something, we got somebody here can find things, anything, lost things."

"Jesus, Johnny. Shut up."

"Tell 'im about Myrna Gresha. Hey, Dutchman, take it easy. We got somebody here who…she found a kid once…she found money…she found water for people's wells… Will you tell 'im before he brains me? Look at 'im. He's nuts. Hey, my brother'll tell you about this woman lives not far from here and she…she cleans people's homes and she… Call her up. Tell her about the short blonde…"

"Shhhhh!" Van Loon hissed like some great snake, and he raised the board. He was about to smash it onto the table, in order to bring order and silence to his tilting porch, but Johnny Fanucci saw murder in the big man's fist, and in Van Loon's eyes he mistook desperation for rage.

"Shit, I'm gone." Johnny walked away quickly, shaking his head all the way to his truck, then hopped inside and drove away. Carl stared at Van Loon, until the man brought his eyes to him.

"Sorry about the hairs," Carl said. "Maybe they're on the floor." Both men stared at the floor, and then Van Loon went to his knees to look more closely, still holding the split floorboard. "Sorry," Carl said again.

"She...finds tings?" Van Loon was still staring at the floor. "Da cleaning woman."

"Oh...well...mostly that was a long time ago. She's weird, and they say she knows what you're thinkin', so people don't like to look at her. It's mostly superstition, but she used to find things. She got sent away for a while. Prison. People don't have much to do with her except...the cleaning."

"She finds...people?"

"Well, I don't know. Maybe. Sometimes."

Van Loon brought his great head up slowly, staring at Carl, who saw the longing there.

"Will you haff her kom here?"

"Who? Myrna? Well..."

"Haff her kom here to clean. Please."

"Well, I guess I can talk to her."

"Tank you." Van Loon rose with effort and stood and looked at the board in his hand and placed it on the table. The pain in his eyes was bottomless.

"I'll fix up this place good for you, Loon. If you want."

The sign painter nodded.

"I got to measure everything and come up with a price, break into a few walls, check it out. I can come back and do that another time if you..." The older man nodded again. "But..." Carl hesitated. "If it's okay...before I go...I'd like to take another look at that painting."

Van Loon stared a moment and then limped away from him, and Carl didn't know if he should stay or go because the sign painter looked so wretched. He decided to walk off the porch, and he was halfway to his truck when he saw the older man coming out of the house, his arms spread wide, the girl-in-the-jungle painting rocking in his hands as he limped toward Fanucci. He stood before the younger man, whose face was all question, and Van Loon made an answer with a nod and with an inch of motion, moving the painting toward Fanucci, who took it delicately. "You mean…?"

"For helping me…wit da cleaning woman."

Carl wanted to give the man a great cascade of thanks, but Van Loon was limping back to his house, thinking that he would live with only one of Greta's oils, the best one, and he would let go of the jungle and the girl because she had been tarnished now by the stream of words from the roof man, and because he knew she would be honored and even revered in the home of Carl Fanucci.

— . —

HOURS later as the day dimmed, Van Loon watched the clouds coming in like great gray ships, and he prayed against the rain, but it came, and by full darkness his roof was leaking into three paint buckets and he was trudging through the storm to the cabin site in waterproof jacket and hat, sending his flashlight beam across the wet, shining shrubs and trees. He stood on the tarped floor and moved in slow circles, searching and waiting and then, finally, calling out to her, "Kom! Kom now! Will you kom?" He didn't see her and heard nothing but the rain pummeling the ground. He thought of walking back to his house, but couldn't make himself begin. He pulled one tarp off the ground and sat on the dry one, holding the first over his head as he stared into the darkness and began calling her again. "Will you kom inside? Will you kom inside my house? Kom inside wit me!"

The rain assaulting the tarp deafened him. He lay down beneath it, feeling like an animal that had burrowed beneath the earth and feeling like an aging man being carried off by delusion and a mad hunger for what he had tasted and what was now denied. Where were the long hairs? How could they disappear? Had they ever been there? Did he dream them? He lay there for an hour until the battering of the rain became so constant it took the place of silence, and he rolled over onto his stomach, face cradled on his arms, and he slept. It was only a moment of sleep, or it may have been hours when she came to him, suddenly appearing beneath him, as if materializing out of the earth itself, and he awoke, terrified at first, feeling her rise up under his bulk and burrow into him, clinging with fingers that were hard as claws through the back of his jacket.

He held her to him as she cried out in her half-shrieking whimper, frightened, forlorn, and he gripped her more tightly, and she wrapped her legs about him, her purpose not sex but safety, afraid of something, maybe the storm, the rain roaring, exploding on the tarp above them. He lifted her slowly as he brought his knees under him. They rose up under the tarp like a sudden growth from the cabin's earthen floor. He stood with her gripping him, her arms and legs and head pressing hard against him.

The tarp slipped off them, and the cool rain found them, and he felt her skin slicken with it, and he said, growling over her head, "Inside! Inside my house!" He turned toward the house and began to move, tripping on the fallen tarp but not falling, stumbling forward, still holding her. He moved as quickly as he could through the storm and saw the light from his windows and pressed her somehow even closer to him as he made for that beacon like a sailor in a heavy sea.

Closer to the house the tangled growth gave way to sparse weeds, and he made a slow, lumbering run that dipped with his limping and brought them into the window light, nearly to the door. As the light fell on them, he looked down at her, so white in his arms, thin but strong, her hair catching some of the gold of the lamplight, and she looked up at him, and he gasped, not from fear, but wonder, the sight of her face making her, finally, plainly real, an angular face, handsome, older than he thought, mouth slightly open, teeth irregular, one missing on the side, all of this in one glimpse, and he saw her eyes on him and some question, some wanting, some fear, some… And then she was gone, and he stopped and nearly fell, a man alone outside his house, gripping himself, standing in the window light under a hard, blind rain.

He stood a while, his arms dropping to his sides, his head revolving slowly, looking for her and knowing he would not find her. In a while he limped heavily to his door and walked up the rotted steps and entered his home, stopping there in the hall, pausing with a new hope—that she was inside now, that she would appear here and he would be greeted now, a man coming home to his woman. He stepped into the living room and saw it vacant, but not empty. It felt to him like a room someone had left just a moment ago so that it held the echo of a presence and this lifted his hope, and he moved into the hall and limped on toward his bedroom, noticing that the door was half-open and trying to remember if he had left it that way, hope turning to a thrilled expectation as he reached the door and pushed it softly, swinging it wide. She would be in the bed, waiting.

He stood in the empty bedroom, stared at the empty bed. He was alone, but he had held her. He still felt the weight of her body. He had not dreamed her. She had a face. She was distinct and individual. He could not have dreamed that face, that particular face, that missing tooth. He was not insane. He was not. He was visited by a spirit, a ghost, a goddess, a demon. He did not know what she was, but she was.

— · —

HE was finishing the sign for the veterinarian when she came, painting the last of the corner figures, the macaw, painting it from memory in colors so vivid they screamed, and he didn't hear her car or her steps until she walked onto his porch, and then he straightened in a sharp jump as she said, "Mr. Loon, I'm Myrna Gresha. Come about your house."

Myrna was small and straight-backed, his own age, with short gray-black hair and a face that had been delicate and pretty and was now diminished not by the etched lines but by the burden in the eyes and the hardness at the mouth. He rose slowly and stiffly from his table, his body aching from two nights spent on the earthen floor of the cabin site with no sign of the blonde woman except her brief mournful cry. His hair, far too long now, was uncombed, and he had not changed his clothes, and his eyes burned with a longing that made Myrna almost turn away.

He tried to penetrate her with this stare, searching for some sign of help and hope, while she studied him as if he were a page and she a slow and careful reader, so neither spoke. She had made her opening remarks, and it was his turn to respond, but he had put aside so many words. They were lost to him, and some of them he missed. He had not said "welcome" in a very long time, and he would probably never say "pleasure" again, though he had liked the feel of the letters in his mouth. Maybe he would say "relax" once more. He would look for an opportunity, but for now he only nodded, and he walked into his living room, and she followed. He sat in the chair, and she stood until he nodded her onto the sofa where she remained stiffly on its edge, looking about at the disordered room.

When her host seemed hopeless in his silence, she offered: "Needs a clean-up. I can smell mildew."

"Der will be…a new roof."

Into the long following quiet, she dropped the words: "Seen your signs around town. I like 'em."

"Tank you."

And then the silence gathered and pooled again.

"It's five dollars if you want me to start." Another pause. "Shall I start?"

Finally, he nodded, and she rose, sweeping everything with her gaze and stopping on the single painting, the Dutch harbor, a fanciful harbor, based loosely on Rotterdam, the late light falling in slabs on the waterfront, moored boats, people and old autos. He followed her look and moved toward the painting, coming to stand beside her, his shoulder taller than her head. He raised a thick, paint-smeared finger.

"My sister…painted us. We are all here. Me." He pointed out a hulking figure walking along the wharf, a two-inch young man, seen from the back. "And herself." Greta was on a bicycle, smiling. "Our brudder." A teenage boy at the run. "Fodder." This man was tipping his hat to a woman who stood in a door-way and waved in return. "Mudder."

"Well, look at that. Your sister's a good painter, ain't she? Yes, she sure is." She glanced at Van Loon with the makings of a smile that didn't hold, and then seemed to stare beneath his skin. After a moment she scouted the room again and looked toward the cluttered kitchen with a professional glance. "It's all kinda helter-skelter. You'll have to tell me where everything goes."

But he told her nothing and only gestured for her to pro-ceed, to move on toward the kitchen. He didn't follow. She walked into the tumble of open boxes and half-unpacked belongings. The cabinets had been repainted and were dry and ready to receive, and she stopped in mid-step, her businesslike mouth loosening and falling open. On each cabinet Van Loon had painted not a word but a picture—of a stack of dishes, a pot, a glass, a can and jar, and these were bright-colored shining cartoons with rounded dimensions that asked for her fingers, as though she could touch them and lift them from their repose. The room smiled at her and welcomed her, and Myrna sent a long sigh into the stillness. The signs on the cabinet doors weren't for him. She knew this. They were there to speak to her so that he could be silent, and her long sigh was for that, for the big hermit who lived in the cave of himself.

He was still staring at the painting as she turned and walked back into the living room and put her gaze on the harbor again and its population, studying with him for a silent half-minute.

"You sure like quiet."

"Peace," he said, a word that he retained as a keepsake, and they studied the painting another long while.

Her eyes narrowed a bit on the figure of the man tipping his hat, and she made up her mind to speak what she learned from the image and from the eyes of the tall man beside her. "Your daddy jumped off a bridge." She said this conversationally. "He didn't know you were still lookin' at him when he jumped. He thought you went away, but you had turned back, and you saw 'im go over."

Van Loon was staring at her with widened eyes and no breath at all. His words, when they came, were half strangled. "He...tol' you dis? My fodder...he...?"

But she was shaking her head. "No. No. I got no truck with the dead. No, *you* did, 'cause you were thinkin' it so hard. I don't hear anything from the ones gone. I just see what's on in people's minds, what they ain't sayin', what they keep so hard. Your mama died in bed. Brother's gone, too, right? Sister's far away. I hope she's still paintin' 'cause she's very good, ain't she? So...Mr. Loon...am I here to clean your house?"

Her mouth was businesslike again, her chin raised as they stared on and on at each other.

"Yes."

"And that's all?"

His large, shaggy head shook a slow, silent negative, and she waited. "You know tings. You...find tings...people."

"I just clean houses now."

"Der is a woman. A woman...comes here...maybe a ghost."

"I don't know nothin' about ghosts. I don't trouble with that. People say things about me, but I don't do that. There's a woman in town who's after me now 'cause her daughter just smashed up her car and died, on purpose, and the mother wants to say goodbye to the girl and tell her she's sorry, but I won't do that say-ance thing, and she said she'd pay me big money, but I won't trick people..."

"But will you just stay...in the dark? Just...watch. She comes...maybe. You just...watch."

"I don't know nothin' about that, and I can't stay late. I'll just clean if you want. It's five dollars. You want me to clean?"

He tried to speak but the effort collapsed, and she saw his old loss and new loss, a lifetime of it. He nodded for her to stay, to clean, but she didn't turn away.

"You know the police are watchin' you? You know that? You were naked at your neighbor's fence, and they say you chased that Johnny Fanucci off your place with a hatchet, he told the police, so they're watchin' you, and they watch me, too. You ever been locked up? You don't want to be locked up, do you? So don't go around naked and tellin' people about ghosts."

His gaze hung on her like a great weight, and she sensed words coming and was patient.

"Why…were you locked?"

"Woman hired me to find some lost money, buried money, and I found some of it, and she paid me almost nothin', so when I found the rest I kept some. She said I stole it. But I found it. It ain't none of my business, but you better watch how you act around people. I'll get to work now."

She had come late in the day, and it was nearing twilight when she finished emptying all the boxes and filling the cupboards and washing the floor and cleaning years of grime and whole cemeteries of insects from the windows. She was hungry and tired and began to search out Van Loon, but he was gone from the porch. She stopped to admire the sign for the veterinarian with its living animals and its line of roses that she could almost smell, and then went looking through the overgrown property.

She found him seated on a tree stump, watching the darkening sky. She noticed that there was a chair nearby, carried out from the house, and she noticed a kind of bed on the ground in the ruin of what had been a small house.

"I'm done in," she said. "I can come back Monday and give you the full day. The kitchen's all done and the floor washed."

He nodded without taking his eyes from the sky.

"So that's five dollars."

He had a five ready in his back pocket and handed it to her. "You are hungry?" he asked.

She said, "Yes," with some wariness.

"You saw der is chili?"

"I saw it."

"Will you heat it? Bring it? Wit da bread. We eat here?" He nodded toward the chair. She considered this and decided she would stay and have her dinner beside him in the chair, and she would do this for him, for the man who had painted the cartoons for her and the man who, when he was young, had watched his father give up and go over a bridge. She walked away while he waited and watched the sky and willed it to be dark.

She returned with their dinner stacked on a wide oven pan, since there was no tray. They ate the canned chili in silence except when she said, "I can't stay late," and he only nodded.

She mopped her bowl with bread and chewed and drank the cool well water and gestured with the glass toward the bed of tarps and blankets. "You sleep there?"

After an overture of nodding, he said, "She koms…there."

She stared at him, and when he turned to her she saw the truth behind his eyes, saw it all with the gift of her knowing. "Jesus, Mary and fiddlin' Joe!" She shook her head and looked again at the cabin floor. "She comes to your bed. And you have sex. And she's a ghost. Fiddlin' Joe in a box!" She began shaking her head again and kept it up as she stacked bowls and spoons and glasses in the pan. "I got to go now," is what she said, but the shaking of her head added that she thought Van Loon was crazy after all, and it was no business of hers.

When she had traveled eight steps on her way to the house, the outcry came, the frightened and plaintive whimper, louder than the birds, and it stopped her and chilled her. It was a woman's voice, and Myrna made a slow circle, studying the trees and thick wild berry bushes, searching with her eyes and with her powers and finding nothing but wonder and impossibility. She returned to Van Loon silent and breathless, and she placed the pan on the ground and continued to scout through the falling darkness, until he asked her, "You could...find her? Please?"

"No." She answered quickly and with certainty, and then said it again. "No," because she knew, somehow, that this was not a voice that came from a place, but from a raw feeling in the air, a torn, misplaced sorrow between the air and the earth.

She watched the darkness and held her breath until he said, "Maybe...she will kom," and then spoke a word to her that he had been holding and saving like a card to play. He said, "Relax."

She took her seat on the chair, on the rim of it, a great distance from relaxed. The wind faltered and died and the dark crept in between their breaths, undetected until it was settled around them, and the sky was a rich black skin, and then she came, and Myrna jumped to her feet and Van Loon rose slowly.

The small blonde woman had been not there, and now she was suddenly there, with her back to them kneeling on the cabin floor, her thick, mussed hair falling to the small of her bare back, her skin very pale, but alive, alive above the bones and the muscles that were beginning to move as she hung her head low and leaned forward and moved her hands on the earth and made her outcry again, and Van Loon gasped, and Myrna turned and ran, stepping into the pan of dishes and spoons, creating an explosion of sound and breakage as she stumbled on through the dark, through branches and bushes, making her way to the house and around the house to her car and entering and turning on the engine and driving for home, while Van Loon stared at the empty ruin of the cabin, the night around him shattered like crockery, the woman gone, and he called out, and Myrna heard him from the road as she drove away, and his neighbor heard him from her porch. "Kom back! Kom back now! Will you kom back?!" But the small woman of pale flesh that stretched across true muscle and bone and moved with life did not appear.

—.—

THREE days later, when Myrna returned home from the cleaning of the Schaefer house, there was a police car parked nearby. She stiffened, but pretended not to notice and pulled into her gravel drive and walked on the broken flagstones to her front door, hoping she would not hear the officer leave his car, but she did. She stood on her step with her hand on the doorknob and waited. She didn't want him inside.

"Hey, Myrna."

"Yes, sir?" She spoke in a tired way, and still had some Kentucky in her sounds, while Chet Goren was crisp about his speech and his uniform. He narrowed his gaze on her face, but she saw enough of his eyes to read a full report on what the man was thinking and what he was hiding.

"What've you been up to?"

"Cleaned the Schaefer's today."

"Uh-huh. Cleaned them out? I heard you were fired by Mrs. Nolan 'cause you took something."

"Never took nothin'."

"Uh-huh. Says you took a ring."

"Her daughter took it."

"You saw her take it?"

"No."

"Well then."

"Nobody saw me take it, neither."

"Yeah, Myrna, but you got a record. You're an ex-convict. I hear you clean now for that Loon—that sign painter."

"One time. Don't know if I'll go back."

"Sure. You go on back—and you tell me what he's up to. He's this close to Elgin State Mental Hospital, you know."

"Don't know nothin' about it."

"Uh-huh. Well, we're talking to a judge about him. He hollers every night. I heard 'im myself. People are afraid to give him work anymore, and he showed up at Tip Top and wouldn't say a word. Looks like hell, too. We know he's dangerous 'cause of him chasing Johnny Fanucci with a claw hammer, so you go and clean his house and tell me what's going on with him."

"It's none of my business."

"It's police business, and you're helping us out, and maybe

I won't press you about that ring if you come back and tell us how crazy he is."

She stared at the younger man and took a chance and asked, "What's crazy?"

"Myrna, don't get smart with me. You know what crazy is. And if you get smart with me, you could find yourself back in prison before you can say Jack Robinson. Now, I could use some fresh-brewed coffee. It's a long shift."

She kept her hand on her knob, but didn't turn it. She faced him a while before she said, "I'm just not sure what crazy is, Mr. Goren. Maybe crazy is a man who don't want to talk. Maybe crazy is a man who hits his wife with an electric cord, hits her on the back, so the marks don't show."

Chet Goren turned into a statue of Chet Goren without color in the face or breath in the chest. She kept her stare on him for five more seconds and then opened her door and went inside and closed the door and waited. The man did not move for a long while, and Myrna's heart punished her and her hands shook so that she held them one in the other, and, in a while, Chet Goren left her doorstep and walked back to his car and drove away.

Van Loon was in his house dressed to go outside, holding the flashlight, but not moving. He would go only when he heard the fearful whimper of the woman. He had heard it every evening, and gone to spend the nights at the cabin site, and he had called to her, but she had not appeared since Myrna Gresha had seen her. He had not eaten dinner, and knew he should fortify himself for another night spent outdoors, but he remained in his chair, coughing now and then, staring at the floor, at an old, desiccated corpse of a mouse while he spoke to himself.

"Dat mouse. Dis is you, Van Loon. Dis is you waiting here so long you die and you dry and become dust waiting here," and he rose and bent over the tiny corpse and lifted it by its tail bone and carried it to the doorway of the porch and flung it out into the night, and saw, at that moment, the lights of a car through the trees and he followed the lights as they came up his winding, dusty driveway. The car parked and the rusted door creaked open and creaked closed and Myrna Gresha came toward him. He nodded and coughed, watching her come.

She studied Van Loon in the light from his porch and saw that he was more ragged and shaggy and even deeper inside the cave of himself than he had been before, and he was phlegmy in his chest now and watery of eye. Both of them stood wordless a while.

"She come back here?"

"Only…her sound. Maybe…because you are here, maybe she koms. You will stay? Please?"

"I'll take that flashlight," she said, and he hesitated and then handed it to her. "You let me be out there alone this time. Even if you hear her, you just let me be out there unless I call you. All right?"

He slowly nodded and said, again, "Please," and the word was a page of all his hopes.

Myrna found the cabin site and sat on the stump nearby and waited, clearing her mind by letting in all the sounds of the night so that her mind and the night became one space, and she prepared her heart for the shock that might come, and when it came, when the voice of the ghost-woman came in that brief, pleading whimper, the beat of her heart increased, but she did not stiffen, and she forced herself to keep breathing and continue to wait. It was the feeling of a presence that came at first, and the presence had no place, not behind her or in front, but simply some living or half-living addition to the weight of the night, and then she was there, the small woman, trim and muscled in her nakedness, facing away from Myrna, standing in the center of the cabin floor, her mussed hair flowing behind her like a yellow scarf, and Myrna swallowed and felt the breath shake inside of her, but she did not catch hold of her breath, determined to accept, and to offer acceptance.

The ghost woman took one step and then dropped slowly to her knees, and when she knelt, Myrna could see no dirt on the bottom of her feet, the feet of a spirit, and then the woman bent and placed her hands on the earth in that same corner of the floor, and she made her small outcry again, and Myrna spoke, softly but evenly, spoke with words she had not prepared but that came on their own.

"What're you doin' here? Why do you come here?"

The woman remained on hands and knees.

"You come here, and you make him crazy. What d'you want?"

The woman didn't move or seem to hear or take any notice.

"You shouldn't come here and make the man so crazy he sleeps out here. He's too old to sleep on the ground out here, and now he's got a cough. You go away." Here she stamped her foot on the ground and spoke in a harsh whisper. "Go away now!"

The ghost woman was there and then not there, and Myrna didn't know if she had chased her away or if she left because Van Loon could be heard now lumbering toward the cabin site, cracking branches and crushing dry weeds.

"Where is she?!"

"Gone."

"But she was here!"

"Yes."

"And she spoke?! I heard a voice!"

"She didn't talk."

He searched the darkness with widened eyes, and then turned back to Myrna. "You spoke?"

"Yes."

"But she did not answer?"

Myrna stared a while more, and then she lied to the man. "I heard her thoughts."

He stepped closer, looming above her in the light of the just-rising moon, his moist eyes eager for what Myrna would tell him.

"Well...Loon...she said she don't like your yellin'. You should stop yellin' for her. It keeps her away."

"She...said dis?"

"Thought it. She thought it. I seen it on her face, y'know, like I do. In her eyes. She don't want that yellin'."

He looked at the ground then and nodded.

"And she...wants to see you better."

"To...see me?"

"She can't see you—'cause a' your beard and your hair so long and messy." Myrna held her breath then, wondering if she had gone too far, but in a while he spoke to her like a young boy. "All dis she said?"

"Thought. She was thinkin' it."

"About...me."

"Thinkin' about you. Yeah. About your face."

In a while he nodded again. He was pleased. "Wat else?"

"Nothin' else. She heard you comin' and just..."

Again, he scanned all the nearby trees and shadowy bushes, so Myrna added, "She ain't comin' back tonight."

"You know dis?"

"Yes I do. I feel it strong. You can sleep inside tonight."

He considered this during a long sigh. "And...tomorrow?"

"Well...I'll come back here to clean tomorrow, and then I'll stay and see if I can make her come again. Just let me do it. Let me try it alone again. I'll come tomorrow when you're away and start the cleanin' again."

"When I am away?"

"Yeah. There's a good barber on the main street in Round Lake. Ben's place. Lots of men go there."

"Ah," he said.

— · —

THE next day Myrna cleaned and organized his home while Van Loon waited his turn at Ben's Barber Shop, the glances of the barber and the customers bouncing off of him as if he were a dark rock in the corner. He picked up no magazines, but he listened to the radio and closed his eyes, and they could hear him, between their own conversations, quietly humming along to "The Happy Wanderer," and "The Yellow Rose of Texas." When he eased his bulk into the chair, he said, "Short." And, "Also da beard."

"The beard short?" asked Ben.

"Da beard gone."

Ben nodded and cut away and soaped and shaved, and as the face of the ponderous man emerged out of the darkness and into the open, the barber said, "Been thinkin' about a sign."

When the sign painter left the shop and walked down the main street, Barbara, just exiting her beauty salon, stared at him and then quickly stared again and asked, "Is that you, Loon?" He smiled politely and with some embarrassment, but two shops later, he paused at the window of the hardware store and studied the man in the glass, and he asked, in his mind, the same question, and he answered.

"Yes. Dis is me. Dis is da man she asked for, my woman," and he smiled, but the smile faded as he examined the jacket that he wore. It was stained and frayed, and so he crossed the street to Lassiter's Clothing Store to buy a new one so that he would look his best for her.

— . —

Myrna parked her old mauled Pontiac a block away from Tip Top Grocery, not wanting to advertise she was coming. She exited the car and swung the door three times until it stayed closed, then she reached into her pocket to touch the money Loon had given her. He told her he had left a list at the store. Myrna was nervous about her lies to Loon, but she looked forward to seeing him shorn of his wild hair and dense beard. She was not looking forward to entering Tip Top though, because they didn't want her there.

She was not welcome in the shops, and her nervousness quickened her, and she knew she would suffer for that quickening because it brought her anger, and when angry, the faces she saw, the eyes she met, were flung open to her more than usual and she saw beyond what she cared to see. She saw too much.

Here, coming her way on the sidewalk, was Sandra Wenslow, a woman of a farm family who lived out of town, and Sandra was nodding to her very briefly, smiling very slightly, and then walking on, but that was only page one of the Wenslow woman, and Myrna turned to page two and saw why Sandra was holding her right hand straight down and not swinging it as she walked, because inside her mind she was walking with her toddler son, his little hand in hers, her son who was born and died before three full weeks of life and never became the toddler his mother imagined beside her, feeling how the little hand might have felt in her own hand, and then the woman was gone by, and Myrna took in a breath that had some shuddering to it and entered Tip Top.

The owner, Al Carli, was working one of the two registers, and his quick, dark look at Myrna was aimed and fired like a gun, his eyes saying, "Be careful" and "I'm watching you," and it was a mean and pitiless look, because Myrna carried the reputation of a jailed thief. But then she saw beyond his anger to the worry that was running through him, constant as a river, from too much stock and too few customers, and when she pulled her eyes from Al, she saw his son, Freddy, looking at her, too, but his eyes were softer and shy and troubled, and she quickly read the list of Freddy Carli's worries, the concern of a twelve-year-old who was afraid of being embarrassed, and often was, but worried now, too, about his mother home in bed and sick, often sick, and Myrna was surprised to find herself also on Freddy's list, as his eyes dodged away from her and flicked back to the shelf he was stocking, but not before she had seen that the boy was upset because his father had told him to keep an eye on Myrna and tell him if she stole anything, and he didn't want to keep an eye on her, and he didn't want to catch her stealing, and then she turned away from the worried boy and took a step toward the second register, not wanting to talk to the owner, but taking her chances with the girl, Alice Borne, and Myrna waited as big Joe Kosloski, who was already checked out, kept talking to Alice and smiling, hoping to hold her interest because she was pretty and he was lonely, and wondering if maybe she would go out with him, and this thought caused a second thought to come, to always come, which was his worry, his years-old worry, that if he did become intimate with a girl, she might be shocked by the livid scars on his chest and upper arms, shocked and even disgusted by what the war had given him, and Myrna was shouting inside herself, asking, "How do we carry this? How do people carry this awful load of pain and of being afraid when it's so goddamn heavy?"

And now Alice Borne was staring at Myrna and waiting for her to approach the counter, and Myrna had to pause, taking in a long breath and trying to sigh everything out of her, everything she knew, everything she saw, and she did this now for Loon, because the man would be coming home from his haircut and he would be needing his groceries, so without looking directly at the girl, Myrna moved to the counter and said, "I'm here for the Van Loon groceries."

"He's got the right name," Alice said, "'cause he's just as loony as can be. Just look at his list. What am I supposed to do with this?"

Myrna inspected the list, which was not in words, but in pictures, drawings of bottles, jars, cans and produce. She looked from the list of objects to Alice and said, "Beer, sausage, lettuce, tomatoes, onions, sliced ham, bread, eggs and jam. You know that your metal sign's broke out there?"

"That's sliced ham?" Alice studied the picture-list again and said, distractedly, "Oh that letter's been blown down for a year."

"So now your sign says, 'TIT,'" Myrna reported, and Alice dropped her jaw. "Well, it does, with the first 'P' gone. It says 'TITOP.' Better get a new sign, a nice painted one."

When Van Loon returned home, Myrna looked up from her work in order to say, not too proudly, but in an offhand way, that they wanted to talk to him about a sign at Tip Top, but the words were halted by the sight of him, a new man in a new jacket, a younger man with a sensitive face, sensual lips, his skin craggy here and roughened there, and this full, clear look at Van Loon caused her to drop her eyes like a flustered girl, and speak her news into the sink.

Later, as they dined and sipped their beers, he broke the silence with, "When she koms, maybe you will ask her…" He faltered.

Myrna said around her food, "She don't hear me."

He drank and then picked up his halting sentence again, the words limping as if with the man's own gait, "…ask her iff she will kom inside—kom to me inside my home."

This time she stared at him. "Loon, I don't think she hears me."

"But…maybe…you will ask. I will wait. Inside."

By 8:30 that night, Myrna was seated on the stump, waiting in the mixture of falling night and rising moon, while an agitated wind pushed and pulled at the vegetation, and Van Loon, sixty feet away, paced across his tilting porch, stopping only when he heard, between the moaning gusts, the whimper of the ghost woman. He stopped and stood a long while and then moved quietly into the living room, where Myrna had hung the mirror, and studied himself there, running his thick fingers through his shortened hair, doing what he could to look his best for the ghost woman who might appear, who must appear.

Myrna remained in place, gripping a flashlight she had no need of, watching the cabin site as the wind hissed in the trees and the moon rose fully and flooded the scene. This would be her clearest look at the ghost if she came, and Myrna eased herself toward calmness, but could not help but be shaken when the presence appeared, this unnamed thing, for "ghost" and "spirit" were only common worn-out words, but this in front of her was an entity from a world we're not supposed to know and never see except by accidents like this, this moment taking place around her as the unnamed thing moved with sound and dimension. Was it only visible memory, a remembrance of someone, memory given bone and sinew and hair: thick, falling, golden hair?

The entity appeared in her corner of the ruined cabin, facing away and then kneeling as she had before, and slowly bending forward to place both hands on the earth. Myrna stood without meaning to, and she realized she was about to take a step closer to the woman, or the memory of the woman, and she swallowed and whispered, "I just...I want to know why. I want to know why you come here. Can you look at me?" Myrna thought that if the woman turned to her, she might be able to see, to know something of her thoughts, but the woman only looked at the earth, and Myrna came one hesitant step closer.

"Who are you? Some woman...some woman gone crazy all alone in a cabin and dyin' and comin' back for what? For him? You don't do him no good. What're you lookin' for?" She felt herself trembling now, her breath becoming unmanaged and broken. She was nearly beside the woman, staring down at her, at her bent head and pale, moonlit flesh, and she found herself reaching out slowly to touch the woman's golden hair that lay across her bare back, reaching closer, whispering now, "What're you cryin' about? What d'you want? What..."

At that moment the woman turned her face to Myrna, and her face was a real face, a face bunched and lined with wanting, with trying, with trying so hard to tell Myrna why she was there, and then she was gone.

Myrna stood alone on the cabin floor, and slowly came down to her knees and reached out a hand and laid it on the earth, on the spot where the woman had put her hands. She laid aside the flashlight and spread both her palms on this place and then moved them slightly, searching, searching, and then stopping and becoming, suddenly, breathless and completely still. After a long while she sighed and straightened and sat back on her heels and gathered her breath for a shout.

"Loon!" Her voice came out shaken, tired.

"Yes!" She heard the man coming.

"No, you wait. You wait. She's gone."

"She is gone?!" He was still coming.

"She's gone, and you go back. You go back and bring a shovel."

— · —

VAN Loon came with a spade and began to dig where Myrna pointed, the blade cutting deeply into the wet earth, deeper with each plunge, driven down by the man's heavy foot, then scooping up the top soil and the thick nightcrawlers, the blind silver beetles and the clawed roots of weeds. She held the flashlight on the enlarging hole, but the moon itself poured in as he dug the dirt away, and they both tensed each time the spade stabbed down, waiting for the sound of blade on bone, but it was metal that it struck. They stared at each other when the sound came, and then he dug more carefully, and finally with his hands, and in a moment drew a tin box from the soil, drew it out with great strength as if the earth wanted to keep it, and Van Loon roared with effort as he tore the box from the grip of the underworld.

When he held it in his hands, Myrna rose off her knees and watched him try to open the box, but he could not, and she followed him to the house, to the kitchen table, where she spread newspapers and he placed the box in the center. He washed his hands and brought a thin screwdriver out of a drawer of tools that had on its front a painted hammer. Myrna cleaned the box with a rag so that the old and partly-rusted tin glimmered. The box was an eight-inch square, only two inches high. Loon worked the screwdriver carefully, but rust had welded the metal, and the operation took a full five minutes, Myrna watching his strong hands being gentle and precise so that the old metal would not bend or break.

When he lifted the lid, they put their heads close together to stare inside. There were pieces of metal in there, rusted into oblivion, and bits of written-on paper, faded beyond reading, but there were coins, too, and Myrna rubbed one until they could identify a silver dollar from 1846. She held this a while to see if the coin kept any memory of its owner and then tried the three polished wooden buttons, but, again, felt nothing. There was a square of half-decayed fabric that still carried some of its red filigree design, and when Van Loon delicately lifted the fragile cloth, they saw the ivory comb that lay beneath it and a necklace with a pendant that was silver but turned green-black by time.

His thick fingers could not pluck the thin chain from the box so Myrna took it out and laid it across her palm, the pendant hanging down, and she closed her eyes. The silver pendant was a flower, a one-inch rose, fully bloomed, with a gently curving stem. She heard Van Loon's quiet gasp and turned to him. He stared at the tiny flower a long while.

"It is…what I painted. It is da same!" He hurried from the table to the porch. He had delivered the sign to the veterinarian, but his practice sketches were there, where he had first painted the rose he saw in his mind, the rose he would repeat as a border at the top of the sign, the fully-bloomed red with a curving stem, and he returned to the table to show her.

Myrna opened her mouth and said, "Ohhhhh." And then she grasped the chain tightly, looking from the colored sketch to the silver flower, and a slight smile spread from her eyes to the muscles of her face, where few smiles strayed and held, and her voice was soft.

"She was talkin' to you, Loon. All this time. Maybe that's what her little cry meant. That little cry. She was tellin' you her name." And Myrna let the silence gather, and then said it. "Rose."

He stared in wonder and in a moment held out a flat hand, and Myrna dropped the necklace there, and he continued to study the silver flower, his mouth forming the name silently. "She will haff it now…when she koms. She will haff all she wanted. Here…in my home. Her treasure."

"Loon…I don't know. I feel like she's gone."

"Gone? No." He was gathering the bits of Rose's history and placing them carefully in the box. "No…she wants dis, so much, and I haff it for her."

"Maybe…maybe she just wanted to be remembered, Loon. And now she will be."

"No." He was more insistent, but not angry, still so pleased. "No, she will kom for dis."

"Maybe she…"

"She will come for dis." He was smiling and certain. "She will kom for dis and for me. She wanted to see me. To see my face! She has not seen me like dis. Remember? She will kom."

She felt guilty then, for her lies. He had believed her so deeply, like a child. "I just…I got the feelin', when she went away this time…I got the feelin' it was forever."

"No! You say you felt dat?"

"Yes, I…"

"No!" His voice was too big for the kitchen now, spilling out into the windy night, and she was afraid. "No! You never felt *her*. Did you ever feel her? Did you ever touch her?"

"No."

"Den you don't know! You don't know!"

"I guess…maybe I don't."

"I felt her. I touched her. I carried her here! Look! Kom!" He went to the front door and outside, and she followed, and the wind pushed at them as he pointed to the ground, just six feet from the doorway. "I came wit her here! Dis close to my

home! Here! Almost inside, and now she will kom. See? See?"
And he went back inside the house and again she followed. He
went into his bedroom, the bed cleaned and made by Myrna,
and on one of the freshened pillows he placed the ivory comb of
the woman named Rose. He laid it there carefully, and then he
walked back to the open bedroom doorway and on the knob of
the door he draped the necklace with the rose pendant hanging
free, and he said, "You see?" And then he went down the hall
and returned to the front door and stepped into the windy night
again, placing the box on the threshold of his home, placing
her treasure there as Myrna watched him.

He only glanced at her, and then walked away toward the
shrubs and trees that were being pawed by the strong wind,
and he disappeared into shadow. In a moment, she heard him
calling out.

"Rose! Rose!"

And Myrna covered her mouth and knew then that she had
done harm and no good at all.

"Rose!"

She followed him and stood near him at the cabin site.

"Rose!"

"They hear you, Loon. They all hear you yellin'—your
neighbor and the cops…"

"Rose!"

"Loon…Loon, sometimes people just go away. They just
go. They're finished and they go." He was not looking at her,
only scanning the shadows, but she went on. "My husband…it
got so he was afraid to look at me, afraid I knew all his thoughts,

everything, and I didn't, but he went back to Kentucky, long time ago, and he never…never came to me again, Loon. People just…"

"She will kom! She will kom to see me. She will kom to have her tings that she wanted so much she cried. She will kom because…it is right! You do not know! Everyone has left! Always! Everyone! So dis is right! *Er moet een balans zijn!*" He was shouting now, to her and into the wind, all the vocabulary that had escaped him now rushing back, filling his throat. He nearly choked on his glut of words. "Der must be balance! For everyone going—somebody here! Balance! You see?!"

"Yes," she said, "yes," speaking to his pain, but he wasn't listening.

"Dis is right! Dis is fate! *Zij is mijn lot!* She is fate—for me! Someone here! Someone to be with me here! You see?!"

"Yes."

"You do not know!"

"I don't. I don't know for sure, but…"

There came a sound then, inside the many voices of the wind as it tore at the vegetation and the boards of the house, and it could have been her outcry, Rose's cry.

"You hear?"

"I think that was…"

"She is koming!"

"Could've been the wind…"

"No! You watch!"

"I can't. I can't be here with you. I can't!" Myrna began backing away. Van Loon stood in the center of the cabin ruin, certain and waiting, and Myrna could not watch him anymore. "I'm goin', Loon." He glanced at her only once as she stepped back into shadow and disappeared, and then he stood alone and scouted the forest and the ground near the remains of the cabin, and not even the wild wind could move him.

He stood as a man waiting for his lover, his face shaved and hair shorn, wearing his new jacket, listening for her step, watching for the sight of her. "Rose," he said, not shouting it this time, but only getting used the sound and the feel of it. "Rose."

He stood for nearly an hour before a cry came again, half-heard within the ransacking of the wind, and he held his breath. Was that his Rose? He waited, and in a moment there was a sound outside his house, something moving. He left the site of the cabin, thinking, "Of course, why would she come now to the cabin?" and telling himself, joyously, that he was a fool. Of course she would not come there. Her treasure was no longer buried there where she couldn't touch it. It was in his home. It was waiting there for her, and she would see it now after so many years, and she would smile and never cry again, and she would see him, see his face, and she would want him, and she would need him, him, Van Loon, whom nobody had needed for so long.

He was moving around the house, when the front door banged against its frame. It was open. He had closed it when he had laid Rose's box on the threshold. It was open and banging in the wind. The box was gone. Gone. He stepped inside, eager but afraid to hurry. He moved down the dark hall toward the bedroom, and the wind blew through the open windows and the moon shone and the trees threw shadows as they danced, and he saw that the pendent hanging on the necklace on the knob of the door was moving, swaying, and he took the last steps very slowly toward the bedroom and felt his breath shuddering inside of him. He swallowed and he whispered, "Rose," and walked into the room as if entering another world, staring at the bed and the living form there, outlined by the moonlight, a small woman's form, and he had no breath at all as he walked to the bedside and waited for the dance of moonlight and shadow to reveal the face on the pillow, and it was revealed, and it was Myrna's face.

Myrna Gresha was in his bed, undressed, the blanket to her bare shoulders. She was staring at the ceiling with moistened eyes, and then, suddenly, darted her gaze to him. Her chin trembled and she opened her mouth, but had to swallow, and then she said in a quick, breathless voice, "You just say so, and I'll go."

He stared at her and blinked and then began to breathe again, as he examined this amazing sight, studied it deeply for a long moment, slowly absorbing it, as slowly as ink moves and spreads into paper, while she brought her dark wet eyes off his face and put them back on the ceiling.

He stood over her like a giant, his gaze on her small form under the bedding, and then moving to her clothing piled neatly on the floor, the ivory comb on the top of the pile. His great sigh was a whole book, the sigh of his lifetime, and he lifted his stare from her and slowly walked away. He moved around the bed and sat on the other side as she stared above. He sighed again and worked his feet against his shoes until they dropped. He lay down on his back and stared at the ceiling along with Myrna. After a long moment she spoke again.

"You just say, and I'll go. You just…"

And he sent a heavy hand to land gently on her bare shoulder, and he said, "Shhhh. Shhhhh."

She hoped his hand would stay, the warm weight upon her small bony shoulder, and it stayed, but she needed to speak just once more, in a whisper this time.

"You just say, and I'll…"

And the man said again, "Shhhhh," and his heavy hand patted her twice, softly, and was left there, and lay still upon her skin.

Reunion

THE LAKES OF NORTHERN ILLINOIS are spread like an unclasped necklace of irregular stones, opal and aquamarine, across a landscape table-flat and rich for farming. These lakes were named for shape: Round, Long, Crooked; for wildlife: Duck, Fox, Deer; and for people and plants and god knows what: Grays, Grass, Indian, and Wonder.

On a Friday in June of 1989, a BMW convertible sped from Chicago toward the scattered lakes, driven by Fred Carli, a man of 48 years, who had been born and raised in Indian Lake, graduated from its high school, and then two years later left and never returned until this particular Friday in June. He was coming back for the thirty-year reunion of his graduating class, the class of 1959, but that's not the whole story.

Four days before, he had flown from his home in Minnesota to attend the graduation of his daughter from the University of Michigan, and that had put him just one short flight from Ann Arbor to Chicago and an hour-and-a-half drive northwest to Indian Lake in time for his reunion, but that's not the whole story, either.

Fred had been to Chicago many times on business, but he had never taken the ride to Lake County, and he was taking it now, and he didn't know why. He had no family there, and he had not kept in touch with anyone from high school. A colleague had passed through the region, through Libertyville, and seen the notice for the reunion and asked him, "Isn't that the little town you're from, Indian Lake?" And he had said yes, it was, and now he was going, and he had no solid reason. Somehow, he needed to see the town, and the store his family used to own, and the old house, the roads, the channel, and the lake. He was driven to do this. It had to do with memories, he supposed, but not with any specific memory. It was more a general weight of remembrance that had come to settle on him like a shirt, and he had carried it with him for weeks, distracted and sleeping poorly and coming to feel that there must be something he had left behind in Indian Lake that he needed to find, and that's the story.

He had grown tired of killing time in Chicago and was driving toward his old hometown one day early, the day before the reunion. He was speeding with no need for speed, the wind playing roughly with his hair as the scenery emptied of buildings and the farms began, the topography of his childhood, the long unbroken fences, the crops, the small gatherings of cows, some of them watching him pass, and to these he shouted through the buffeting wind, "Hello, how you doing? Used to live here! I knew your grandmothers!"

— . —

HE had booked no place to stay and had no memory of any hotel in or near the town. He chose a motel just a few miles before the Indian Lake limits because it looked new and clean, even sterile, and that appealed because he did not want to mingle, not until the reunion. He wanted only to gather images of his past and think his thoughts. He rented a room for two nights and brought in his bags and looked at himself in the mirror. He was tight and even pained around the eyes, so he eased the muscles of his face and took in a deep breath and tried to expel all the tension he carried like cigarette smoke on his clothes, all the stress of being around his ex-wife and her new husband as they hovered near his daughter and made shallow conversation when she wasn't with them, and then the graduation dinner with all of them around the table had not gone well because he couldn't relax and so had taken one or two drinks more than he should have, not enough to be drunk, but enough to catch both looks, the look of his ex-wife that sent him a kind of faded disappointment, and the look from his daughter which was a look of avoidance, not meeting his eyes, not meeting anyone's eyes because she was embarrassed, and he had seen this and tried very hard not to slur a word or raise the level of his voice, which only made it more difficult for him to relax. In fact, he couldn't remember the last time he had fully relaxed. He had not put aside all of his tension, which ran like a small motor or a clock ticking in his chest for… He couldn't remember. He tried to think of the last time he had slept well, the last time he had laughed himself to tears, the last time he had made love all out.

He sat on the motel bed and took more deep breaths. He didn't want to be tense or distracted. He wanted to approach his old home feeling calm and open to whatever would come when he stood before the old place, all the old places, but especially the house where he had grown up, where his mother had died, the house he had left behind only days after the funeral when he and his father had fled their lives and created new ones.

He washed his face and upper body and put on a fresh shirt and smiled into the mirror, but the smile was not for himself. It was a smile of greeting. He wanted to see what they would see, the people he would meet, the people who remembered him. "Hi," he said to the mirror. "Fred Carli," and he studied himself through their eyes. He wore a trimmed full beard and kept his body fit. He was balding slightly, and he looked weary, even after the deep breaths, even with the smile. He stared into the tired eyes and spoke a word not quite aloud. He said, "Pillsbury," and he nodded. "I'm an executive there in PR. Uh-huh, finished college at U. of Minnesota. Right. And how are you?" The people in the mirror were mildly glad to see him and mildly impressed.

He walked outside to the shiny BMW rental and smiled again, but this smile was jaded and wry and aimed at his own vanity. Yes, he wanted them to know he had done well. He wouldn't talk about it. He wouldn't brag, but he wanted them to see it. He made a shrug to absolve himself and pulled out of the parking lot and headed for the town, reviewing his list: the main street, the house, the store, the channel, the lake, and maybe he would add the school, and then see if the A&W Root Beer drive-in was still there—but it wouldn't be, and maybe he'd walk to Buddy Benson's house, just to take the same steps over the same street he'd taken hundreds of times, and maybe drive by Nancy Darrow's house because she had been his first serious girlfriend, and he had been thinking about her, thinking about all the ones he knew well, thinking about the humid, white-hot summers with the sun glaring off the gravel roads and the stones crunching under his shoes, and thinking about the smell of the mud at the banks of the channel, a half-rotted and coppery smell he could still evoke any time he thought of it, and thinking also about Nancy and him on the roomy bench seat of his old Pontiac Chieftain and their first touchings and then their wild, breathless explorations that shook them and amazed them and scared them, too, thinking about all of it and wondering where it might be buried, this thing, this moment, this feeling he needed to find.

He rolled into the town and was glad to see the old water tower and the small railroad station, but the department store had a new name and a new façade, and the volunteer fire station was gone and the small park, too, and there were new businesses that were already old, a video store, a pizza place, a laundromat, and a bar that had only one small, glass-bricked window and its name painted on the cinderblock wall, RON-NIE'S, its door losing its finish, and all of this not mattering because it was the kind of bar only regulars entered, and Fred rolled by in his convertible, not belonging to any of this. He was disappointed, not because the town had changed, but because he felt nothing for what was left of it, and he wanted something, at least nostalgia, to begin to kick in like a first drink and spread through him.

He drove toward the channel, noticing the water glinting between houses and watching for a side road to the banks, thinking the layout of the streets must have changed, most of them gone to chip-seal now instead of gravel. He stopped at an empty lot that had a footpath though the overgrown stickers and berry bushes, and he braked the car and looked about and then left it and walked down the worn path, raising dust that coated his loafers.

He came out of the bushes at the channel banks, and the quiet water, sliding its slow way to the lake, calmed him. He walked to the water's edge and breathed in deeply and smiled because the smell was there, the same coppery smell, and it gave him the connection he was waiting for, and the memories came and crowded around him, all the afternoons fishing here, sitting and watching his plastic bobber and dreaming here, and he began to feel more inside the skin of the boy who was himself, all the boys, the little ones and the teenagers who were himself.

He sat on the bank as if to enter the boy who was him and imagined himself at…about twelve, tried to feel it, the different perspective, the ease in his smaller body, the absence of any claim on his time, the thoughts he might have been thinking back then, right here, on this grass and these weeds that had died and grown again for so many summers, but he may have thought too long and gone too deep inside his memory because he began to rediscover the thoughts of the twelve-year-old boy, his eyes may have been on the bobber, yes, but his mind was working over the possibility that his mother was getting sick again, and what if that made his father start drinking more, not that the man needed an excuse, and would he let the store falter? And what if…?

He found himself on his feet again, taking a long breath and expelling it along with it the memories he didn't want.

He walked along the bank, slowly, taking in the sun and the heat and trying to make that enough, without searching for anything. He reached the small bridge and crossed to the other side, moving along slowly, letting himself hear the hum of the yellowjackets and study a red-winged blackbird on a willow branch. He hadn't seen one for years, the vivid scarlet patch on the blackest black, and he watched it preen and then fly off, lifting him a bit.

He took his time walking back to the car, taking one more long draft of the scent of it all, the channel and its reeds and its mud, and then he saw the man, parked in the middle of the road, staring at his BMW and now at him. The man eased out of his pick-up truck, a tall, thin man, shaven head and dark eyes intent on Fred's face.

"Jesus. Freddy?" the man said, and shook his head, as if there was something wrong, deeply wrong that he couldn't understand.

Fred smiled and studied the man's features but could not find a fit with any of the blurred faces of those who populated his boyhood. He put out his hand and said, "That's me," but the man ignored the offered hand, still intent on Fred's face.

"You've got a beard. A full beard."

Fred chuckled then and shrugged. "Sorry, did we go to school together?"

"What?"

"I can't think of your name."

"Jesus," the man said. "Jesus, Freddy, it's Walt Timmel!"

Fred offered his hand again, and Walt looked at it, unsure, and then shook it limply, still caught by a confusion that seemed to be pummeling him.

"Sorry, Walt. I've been away a long while, and the memory, you know, isn't great."

"Where you been?"

"Minnesota."

"No shit."

"Yeah. I work for Pillsbury there, in public relations."

Walt stared a long time and then echoed the word, "Pillsbury."

"Yeah. Minneapolis. What about you, Walt?"

Walt dropped his gaze to the ground, looking more and more troubled, and here Fred began to think that the man was not right in his mind, and he searched his past for the boys he knew from school who were slow, but only remembered the one who had been allowed to graduate and then had stayed at the school on the janitorial staff, because he loved the school, and he came out for every game and even led cheers, but that wasn't Walt.

"Pillsbury," Walt said again, staring at the ground and blinking, hands on his hips.

"Uh-huh. And Green Giant." That brought Walt's eyes to Fred again, and Fred winked at the man. "We just bought Green Giant, too. That's a corporate news flash, Walt. Not even released yet." Gently, Fred touched Walt's shoulder, and then he stepped away, moving to his car. "Maybe I'll see you at the reunion?"

Walt was studying the ground again, looking pained, looking as if he had lost his hold on something, on everything. Fred almost asked him if he needed help, but he didn't want to be sucked into Walt Timmel's problems. He wanted to hold on to the scent of the channel banks and go hunting for more of his past, for more of the boy who used to be him. "Bye, then," he said and started the car and pulled away, seeing Walt in the rearview mirror, still deeply troubled.

He decided to save the house for last and headed for Cedar Lake Road where the store used to be, his mind still moving through the half-remembered mob of boys that had populated his school life, looking for a possible Walt.

He reached the small cluster of old and new businesses that lined both sides of the road, and he slowed and stared and caught his breath. It was still a grocery store, and they hadn't even changed the name: Tip Top Grocery. The sign was still there, the old sign, weathered but otherwise intact, even the façade of the store was nearly unchanged, the large window always a bright chaos of sale signs. His mouth remained open as he studied the details. The doors were automatic now, and there were pictures of credit cards on them, and the parking area was paved, and everything else was the same. No, the store was bigger. It had swallowed the small hardware store next door.

Fred was in the middle of the road, so he pulled over and parked across the street from Tip Top and took it in. He remembered a thousand days and nights all out of order, felt again the strain of heavy boxes against his young muscles, trimmed the produce and wetted it down, swept the aisles, ran the old cash registers with the large keys and the bells, watched his father cutting meat on the slicer, his worried father, and he smelled the salami and the liver sausage, and he carried bags out to the customers' cars, just as a boy was doing now, a lanky boy of sixteen or so, walking behind a woman, following her to her station wagon, waiting and inserting the bags, and it could have been him, thirty-two years ago.

Fred watched the boy re-enter this so-familiar store, still there after decades, looking bright and thriving and somehow eternal. He held his stare, watching as another woman came out, a young woman carrying a bag clutched against her and opening a bottle of water and taking a drink, the bag getting away from her, slipping, and Fred watched it fall and hit the sidewalk and saw her swearing. Something leaked out of the fallen bag, and she did a one-step dance of anger and went back into the store, and he watched all this, watched it happening at Tip Top Grocery, still happening, and then the woman came out again, and a man followed her with a broom and a dust pan, and the man wore a short apron, and was smiling at the woman and talking to her, calming her as he went about the task of cleaning up, and as Fred watched the man, his breath stopped and a chill went through him like a wave, with the force of a strong icy wave, because the man, the aproned man, was himself. Himself. Not someone who looked like him, but him, the self who Fred saw in the mirror every day, and Fred opened his mouth, and his breath forced its way inside of him and shivered in his chest, and he did not believe what he saw, and he could not look away, because it was exactly him, every gesture, every part of his body, and Fred made a small sound as if he had been struck, and he felt tears gather in his eyes and his throat because something was happening, and he must be sick. He must be coming apart. This must be the end of something, of his sanity, his life, and so tears came, but he could not stop watching as the man spread the fallen items on the sidewalk and swept the broken glass into the dustpan and went back inside the store.

Another small outcry came from Fred's throat, and his chin was shaking and the breath shaking in his chest because the man was him, him now, as he looked today, except the man did not have a full beard, only a ragged goatee, and that was the only difference, and all of this was impossible, and Fred sat in his convertible and shivered and silently wept and watched the door, and the man came out again, and Fred made the small outcry again, watching him, watching him move, watching him smile, watching him gathering the items and filling a new bag and handing over the bag with hands that were his own hands, and the woman waved and walked away, and the man who was the same as Fred, *was* Fred, walked back into the store.

Fred sat in his car, his stomach and chest shaking as he swallowed tears and watched the door of Tip Top Grocery, but the man did not come out again, and Fred's fingers were moving, and he wasn't sure why, and then he realized he was pushing at a button with a hand that looked like a palsied hand, the trembling finger missing the button and then finding it, and the top of the convertible rose up from the back and came down slowly and covered him, and he used his palsied hands to fasten it so that he could be hidden from everyone while he thought, while he found out if he was having a breakdown or was completely insane or dying.

He waited for twenty minutes, unable to look away from the automatic doors of Tip Top Grocery, but only customers came out and not the man who was him, and his shaking would not stop or even diminish, so he had to drive away or he would start weeping or crying out at the madness.

He drove out of Indian Lake, not paying attention to his direction, and at the outskirts of the town there was a restaurant beside the highway that was a bright, polished, anonymous chain restaurant where he felt he could stop and hide and gather himself and think this through, or maybe it would just go away, maybe it was a delusion. Of course, it was a delusion, and it would wear off and go away.

He sat in a spongy booth far from anyone and put his elbows on the table and his hands on his eyes. He heard the approach of someone, and heard a glass set on his table, a glass of water he supposed, and he heard a woman ask him, "Coffee?" and he nodded behind his hands, and he heard the pour, and heard her walk away. He removed his hands from his eyes and stared at the steaming mug in front of him, knowing that if he picked it up he would spill it on himself because of the shaking, and then he thought that maybe he should spill it on himself so the shock and the pain would bring him out of this and bring him back to what was real, and he hooked a finger in the mug and lifted it, carefully, and it didn't spill, and he sipped the bland coffee and put the mug down with only a little shaking, and he told himself he was starting to feel better, and that it was only someone who resembled him, and his mind had done the rest and tricked him, and he felt his breathing become more regular, and he cleared his throat to hear the sound of his voice, and now the waitress was moving toward him without a smile, and he made himself ready to talk to her in a normal voice.

The waitress said, "Haven't seen you in here in a while," and he said nothing, his chest frozen again. "Like the beard—full like that," she said. "Want to hear the specials?" He didn't speak or move. "Need a minute?" When he didn't answer, she came closer, and her eyes examined him. "Freddy, you all right?" And here he made a move, because he had to, so she would go away. He gave a slight nod, knowing that he was giving in, that he was accepting the impossibility that there was another him, and that the waitress knew this other him, accepting it for at least this one moment and pretending to be the other him and nodding to her instead of screaming that this was all insane and that he was insane and that she should call a doctor or an ambulance and he should be helped, he should be taken away and helped, but instead, he nodded his head, and this sent her away, and when she was gone, he fumbled with his wallet and placed three dollars on the table and left the restaurant.

— · —

FREDDY Carli, who was the owner of Tip Top Grocery and who had worked in the store since he was twelve and worked there during summers while in college, was a man of forty-eight, with a few gray hairs in his ragged goatee and an easy, vaguely distracted smile. He stood behind one of the two check-out counters, scanning the prices, working the register, but thinking about his high school reunion party tomorrow night where he would go with his wife, and he felt both eagerness for that event and dread. He was also distracted by the steady stare of the next customer in line, a man he knew, who was putting no groceries on the counter and seemed upset and probably had a complaint.

"What's up, Walt?" he asked, when he was finished with his customer and ready for the complaint. Walt Timmel did not break his stare, and Freddy noticed that the man's chin was trembling slightly, so he lowered his voice and asked more seriously, "What's wrong?"

Walt's voice was husky with emotion. "What's wrong is what you said down by the channel, and…how you looked…with your beard. What are you doing? What are you doing, Freddy?"

Freddy stared as if Walt had spoken a dead language. "The channel? What I said when?"

"Down by the channel, about an hour ago. Jesus. Pillsbury! What was that shit about Pillsbury?" The man was terribly angry, but also lost, desperate somehow for answers to his questions, and Freddy could not translate those questions into any pattern that made even a shade of sense.

"Pillsbury?"

"Goddamn it, goddamn it. You're saying you didn't say that to me—about Pillsbury?" Walt could see only a storm of confusion on Freddy's face, and the tall man made a jerky gesture with his hands and shouted, "Jesus!" the word coming out almost tearful, and he walked out of the store, shaking his head, his chin trembling and his eyes wild.

—·—

FRED Carli, the man from Minneapolis, the man who worked for Pillsbury, had driven from the restaurant to his motel, and he was in his room, seated on his bed, staring at the impenetrable problem that life had shoved in his way like a boulder. He thought about the waitress and went over every one of her words, and then he thought about the man named Walt and reran their conversation again and again, and then he made himself see what he had seen at Tip Top, even though it terrified him to see it again, even in his memory. He watched himself come out of the store and speak and move, himself in an apron, himself with a ragged goatee instead of a beard, and what else? Nothing else. It was him, and it could not be him.

He reached for the phone and picked it up and put it down and stared at it, then he reached for the thin phone book on the shelf beneath the nightstand and made himself slap at the gray pages until he was in the Ts, and then found the store, but he couldn't make himself punch in the number. He only stared at it.

He wanted this to be over. He wanted to wake up, and have it be over, but he wasn't asleep, and he couldn't think of a way to end it, and then he thought of a way, and he reached for the phone and waited until a number arranged itself in his memory, and he tapped it in and waited and prayed that he would not get a machine…

"'Lo?"

At the sound of her voice his chest opened and air and warmth moved through him and tears moved into his throat, and he tried to clear them and say, "Hey, Reet," but the words crumbled, and so he said them again, and she answered, with just the thinnest amount of strain.

"Hi, Dad."

So there he was, on one end of a wire that traveled for hundreds of miles through the earth and the air, and on the other end of that wire was his daughter, Marita, and she was speaking to him, and connecting him to the reality that he counted on, that he gripped now so hard his fist went white around the phone.

"Good to hear your voice, honey," he said, and he wondered what she thought of that because he had just been with her two days ago, but all she said was, "I'm really studying here, Dad, so I can't talk long."

"Yeah. Sure. Right. I'm in Indian Lake."

"How's it going?" she asked, but she was only half listening, her hands probably busy with a task, the phone trapped by a shoulder. When he didn't answer, she said, "What's up?" wanting to get to the reason he called, so they could deal with it and she could get back to work.

But he couldn't tell her that he had called her so that she could prove to him that he was real, so he said only, "I just want to congratulate you again."

"Oh, right. Yeah. Thanks for the money."

"Sure. It's for the move and…"

"Yeah, you said. Thanks." She was working in a lab for three more weeks and then moving to California for graduate school, so far away, and he was struck by the vague pain of having his daughter live so far from him, but he was glad, even for the pain, because it was part of the mosaic of his real life, the life he had lived up until an hour ago, the life he would live again, the life he could trust. "I just wanted to hear your voice, Reet."

"Oh." That stopped her. He wondered if he had ever said that before. He couldn't remember. She asked, "Why?"

"Why?" He echoed her question, fumbling for more to say, but she went on.

"I mean, what, you think I'm mad at you? You always think I'm mad at you after, but I'm not mad, so… It's just you, you know? I wish you weren't that way, but you are, so… I'm not mad, and I really thank you for the money, and I really have to get back to work." He heard all the text that didn't appear in her sentences, the hurt and the judgment that crowded between her words like static.

"Reet, I wasn't drunk. I wasn't even close."

"Whatever you say."

"I know what drunk is. I had a drunk for a father so…"

"You told me. I know. You know what I'm going to do with some of that money?" she asked, changing the subject in a turn without a turn signal. "I'm going to rent a trailer 'cause I can't possibly load everything into my car."

He took a long breath. "It's tricky, you know, pulling a trailer," and he was glad to hear himself say this, and even glad for the worry he felt for her on the road with the trailer, because that, too, set him deeply within his normal life.

"I'll be careful. So…"

She used the word, "So" to signal to him that she wanted the call to be over. She had done that for years, but he didn't want to release his grip on the phone and on his life. "I'll call you again soon, Reet."

"Uh-huh. Okay. Bye," and she was gone too quickly, while he was still fumbling for more to say, and he knew that he had lost her again, that he had lost her a long time ago, given up the little girl who had waited for him to come back from his job and his travel and his drinking, and he had never come back enough, not nearly enough, and she had stopped waiting, and he had lost her.

He slowly replaced the phone and lingered with his hand on top of it and waited and then dropped his eyes to the phone book in his lap and found the number again, and feeling strong enough to call now, dialed the store quickly before he could stop himself. He sat waiting for the ring with his heart clanging like some fierce machine, and the voice that answered was a young voice, "Tip Top," and Fred swallowed and tightened his voice and said, "Freddy, please," praying that this would be over now, a vague plea to the universe, sent out there like a missile with no target.

— . —

FREDDY Carli's son, who worked with him in the store, as Freddy had worked in the store for *his* father, shouted, "Dad on one!" and Freddy heard him, but was still talking to Heather Cole about Walt Timmel, wondering if Heather knew what was wrong with Walt, but she didn't, and Freddy said that Walt seemed very pissed off at him, and that's when he picked up the phone and punched line one and said, "This is Freddy."

Fred Carli, seated on the bed in his motel room, heard his own voice on the phone, heard it again as Freddy said, "Hello?" And there was no mistake, and the sound chilled him in every bone, and his eyes closed tightly and his teeth met and pressed, and he did not even move to breathe, and Freddy spoke a questioning hello one more time in the exact voice of Fred, and then hung up.

It was two or three minutes later when Fred replaced the phone and let the book slide off his lap as he rose from the bed. He walked into the bathroom and stared at himself in the mirror, at the outside of himself and through the eyes into his core, and through that into something else, the universe maybe, the core of everything, and though he stared a long time he saw no answer, but he did see what he was going to do, and that surprised him, but he began to do it anyway, taking the scissors from his shaving kit and the brush and brushing out the hair on his cheeks, the hair of his beard, and clipping it off with the scissors.

— . —

FORTY-FIVE minutes later he was seated at the bar of the glass-bricked building, the new saloon in town that was already old, and he was sipping a vodka tonic and looking into the mirror at the self in the glass, studying the loss of his full beard and the shape of the ragged goatee and waiting for someone to tell him who they saw there, but nobody told him, nobody spoke to him at all. He thought that by walking into the world of this madness, like a spy, he might smash it, he might bring it down, and he was vibrating inside, waiting for an explosion. He put his stare on the bartender as she brushed her towel over the splashings of beer near the taps, watched her flipping her head to get the blonde hair off her eyes. "Are you Ronnie?" he asked her, his voice jumpy. He was remembering the name on the wall outside.

"Nope," she said with no smile or even a look in his direction. He spoke again anyway, feeling like an actor saying lines.

"How long have you been in Indian Lake?"

This received a cool blue stare and she told him, as if it were a long time, "Fourteen years," and he dismissed her as a newcomer, feeling possessive about the old town as it used to be. "You?" she asked him,

And he said an odd thing. He said, suddenly, "Ever since

they showed free movies against the wall of the hardware store. In the summer. People brought their own chairs." He hadn't remembered that for decades.

"I remember that," said a roughened voice from down the bar. There were three other drinkers beside Fred, two speaking softly, unheard, and this older man, still nodding. "Yeah. Called it the 'free movies.'"

"Right," Fred said, catching the man's eyes, but the man said nothing else. The man didn't know him. Shouldn't they know him? And what if they did? What should he say? How does he behave? How does he break this apart? He faltered. He wasn't sure of his lines, didn't know the script, and he suddenly wanted to leave.

"Anybody know what time Tip Top Grocery closes?" He looked to his left and right, throwing the net of his question throughout the dim bar, and one of the drinkers said, "Eight, I think," and the bartender said, "There's a supermarket on 83 open till ten." He nodded and paid and walked out of the dimness into the sunlit street that felt like another time zone, and he stood still and surveyed the town.

He saw the barber shop and was walking across the street without thinking about it, without deciding, as if he was following an instinct or maybe just moving blindly like a punched man, reeling. He looked through the wide glass window, and saw there what he had always seen, Ben Zyrnic cutting hair, only Ben was much older, his own hair bright white now, but no difference in his broad girth, in his movements, and the barber glanced through the window and settled his eyes on Fred and nodded, and Fred moved to the open door of the shop and paused in the doorway, as if it were a doorway to a different life. It was just a nod hello, he thought, he doesn't know me either. I don't understand. What happens now?

"You need a trim, Freddy."

Ben said this without looking up from his cutting. The sentence was amazing, the opening of a door. He could walk through. He found he could not speak, not yet, and he did not know what showed on his face, but he was inside now, as he had been on the road with Walt Timmel, and with the waitress in the restaurant. But this time he was inside to stay, until, somehow, he made it fall apart, he made it end. The barber was speaking again.

"Turn around."

"What?" He said that automatically. His first word as…whoever he was, and now what?

"Show me the back."

Fred was frozen, and it felt like breaking himself to move, but he moved, turning slowly in the doorway.

"You've had somebody else at your hair."

When Fred looked again at Ben, he was busy with his cutting, but carrying a smile that wasn't much more than the thought of a smile. "Your wife been snipping at your hair?"

"My wife?"

Ben shook his head as he worked. "Somebody."

Fred stared at the man who had cut his hair from the time he was ten until he was twenty, stared across the ages at Ben Zyrnic, and he spoke to the man as himself and as someone else, too. He made himself say, "Only you, Ben." And then he waved awkwardly and walked away, feeling the strangeness as a kind of electricity. He realized that along with the fear, he was excited. He was two men walking down the main street of Indian Lake. He was Fred Carli who had left twenty-eight years ago and come back today, and he was someone who had not left and who still went to Ben's Barber Shop and who had a wife. A wife.

Someone honked a car horn, and he looked, and someone waved and smiled, driving on, and he waved because he thought he should, and then a woman came toward him, speaking as she neared him and passed him, saying, "Now I hope you have some yellow bananas today in that store, 'cause I hate when they're all green. My family wants 'em every day, Freddy." And he turned around and watched her walk away, and the electric power of this second life was humming inside of him, frightening and fascinating and humming like a motor at the core of him.

He walked to his car and entered and drove around the town, waiting to know what to do, and then knowing and driving to the old house and passing it slowly. The emotion he expected at the sight of it was diminished by the remodeling. It filled its lot now, with only a willow in the corner and no more giant oak and no pines, and it was white instead of brown, with new siding and a different pitch to the roof, and there were flagstones with flowers beside the stones, and he rolled the car along, looking at the other houses now, seeing some that had changed very little, and he drove down a side street and another to come close to his old property from a different direction, and he parked half a block away and exited his car and stood and stared at the house.

It could be inhabited by new owners. It could mean nothing to him, the house where he had been raised and where his mother died, the house he and his father had abandoned could be empty for him now, but he went to it, slowly, and passed through the decorative arch and stepped on the flagstones and onto the cement porch that ran beneath the front windows, its wrought-iron railings painted white and only slightly chipped, and the door asked for his hand with a bronze knocker, and there was a button for a doorbell to the side, but he only stood there and stared at the door, remembering the thousands of times he had walked through, just walked through without a key, without a thought, coming home from school or from work at the store or from a ballgame or from a ride with Buddy Benson or a date with Nancy Darrow, and he would just flow through the door, moving from the world outside into his home with no thought except the thought of what he was going to do next, to eat or to study, or to make a call, or to go to bed, and then the other old thought came, the thought to be quiet, which was not a true thought but an automatic shift into careful movements and hushed speech because his mother was likely to be sleeping if she'd had another bad night, or be resting, or be sick in bed, sick again or continually sick with the dark, tangled mysteries of adhesions and obstructions and blood within the cavities where no blood should be.

Fred stared at the door and through the door into his life

before, and he felt his boldness slipping away as the memories held him there on the porch for nearly five minutes before he heard a sound from inside the house. It jarred and stiffened him, and he stopped his breath to listen. He heard steps, hurried steps inside and then silence, and then the steps again, almost at the run, and his eyes fell to the handle of the door, and he saw that his hand was slowly reaching for it, his thumb depressing the grooved tongue of the lock, and his hand lending its weight, just enough to swing the door open two inches, and he held it there for seconds and then pushed and stepped into the house in blind desperation, as if this action could shatter the all the questions and settle this, settle it.

He stood inside a small foyer that had always been there, but freshened now, its doorway widened, and his hand was still on the door, and he was staring into an enlarged living room, feeling fear and also a sense of wonder as if he were in a dream and aware that he had no control and no idea what might happen, and what happened was that a boy of twelve or so jogged into the living room and jumped jerkily to the side, shouting.

"Oh! Holyholygod, Dad! Shit! You scared me. God!" And then the boy smiled, his mouth and eyes wide. "You shocked me like I almost fainted!"

Fred stared at the boy, who was familiar or at least reminiscent of someone he knew, but he could not think or speak or move, and now the boy was coming toward him, saying, "I gotta go. I'm late. We're all getting a ride from Darryl's mom…" And Fred had to move because the boy was hurrying by him to leave by the open door. "…and Ari's dad is picking us up. See ya!"

And the boy took one step down from the porch and jumped the rest and landed on the flagstones and jogged through the arch and off the property and down the street.

Fred watched the world framed in the doorway, and as the boy passed beyond the frame, the world emptied of people, and there were very few sounds: distant cars, a faraway lawn blower, airplane, birds. He closed the door on all of this, shutting himself inside his old house and turning and stepping into the living room and listening again, but certain, somehow, that the house was empty but for him. It was the way it breathed, and the distant, inhuman buzz of the refrigerator and the soft tick of a clock somewhere nearby, on the mantle, he saw. It was an antique clock and centered above it a mirror, and he walked to the mirror and studied himself in his old house made new, searched his face and found the boy there, the boy he had just frightened, who must be, in some other life, in the life of this house, his son.

He bit the inside of his lip, increasing the pressure of the bite until he tasted blood, but he did not wake up from a dream, and the taste of the blood was as real as the face of the boy, and he looked around the room now, feeling the impossibility of all of this begin to smother him. His glance moved in a ragged circle, finding nothing to attach itself to until it clutched at a tabletop where a framed photo stood beside a lamp, and he was striding across the room, his hand jumping for the photo, a studio shot, a family, and there was the boy he had just seen, and an older boy, the one he had noticed at Tip Top Grocery, the one carrying groceries for a customer, and there was himself, the other himself, the self at the store, Freddy, smiling a smile Fred didn't think he could make. It was soft. It was happy and relaxed, and he didn't think he had that particular smile in him, and beside this other self was her, the wife of Freddy, and he knew her, in spite of the years, and his eyes and his throat filled at the sight of her, at the look she was giving him, the warm joy she gave the camera and through the camera to him, even now, and he loved her, and it was Nancy, Nancy Darrow, who, in some version of his life, was married to him and lived in this house with him and with their sons and breathed the air he was breathing now and moved among the furniture here and filled the room with her voice.

Without any notice of what he was doing, he sat on the edge of a chair and held the framed photo in both hands and stared at each face and lingered, again and again, on the face of himself and on the face of Nancy Darrow, who had been his girlfriend for two years of friendship to the bone and episodes of wild passion without consummation and then, slowly, he had begun to unfasten from her as his eyes drifted toward the larger world, and he went to college and tried to shrug off Indian Lake like a winter coat, shrug off the store and the life here, and then his mother had died, her death breaking his father so that they both struggled out from under their heavy coats of the past and left all of it behind, the store sold, the house sold, and a new life made in a new place, and they took her with them, took her ashes with them and sequestered them there among her relatives where he, where Fred stopped being Freddy, and began to make his new life, and where his father let the drink take him, gave up and let the drink take him and kill him and lay him beside his wife in sixteen years.

Fred looked up from the photo and breathed in deeply the air of the house that carried the scents and echoes of a family that was his and not related to him at all except by some cataclysm of chance, some breaking down of the rules of natural human life. What had happened to those rules? Weren't they unbreakable, like the rule of sunset? Like the rule of death? How could the universe or God or science let this happen, let him be sitting in this house, the house they lived in, they, Nancy, the children, and the other him?

He looked at the photo a moment more, and felt the warmth invade him again, the warmth of her, and then he began to wander through the rooms, watching the life of a family unfolding in the details of crumbs in the kitchen sink and messages on the refrigerator, a cracked window pane, a soccer ball, a long scratch in the paint of the hallway wall.

He stepped into the master bedroom and paused there. The bed was roughly made and there was castoff clothing on the spread, his clothing, hers. The top of a low dresser was cluttered, and there were more photos there, one of the couple, one of the kids, younger, and one that rocked him and rooted him so that nothing moved but his mouth, opening slowly and slackly, and then his throat moved, the liquid nearly choking him there and forcing him to swallow as he emitted a cry that was close to a sob.

It was a picture of the two boys, about the ages they were now, and standing behind them, a hand on each shoulder, was their grandfather, Fred's own father, old and thin and wrinkled and alive. Alive. He wore a wry, twisted smile, and his eyes were clear, and there was joy in them, and he was older than he had ever been allowed to age. Seventy-five, maybe. And Fred had lost him and buried him when the man was sixty-one, and yet here he was in this photograph, at least seventy-five and clear-eyed, and alive. Alive.

It may have been the longest minute of his life before he stepped closer to the dresser and reached out and picked up the photo and studied the aging man and let the tears come and felt the wetness on his face and only swallowed thickly but wiped nothing away and spent the next long minute swallowing and making sounds in his throat. Dad was here. It was all here. The house and a family and the store and even Nancy Darrow, and Dad was alive, and it was all here.

It was an endless amount of time or it was no time at all, and he was walking through the house again and out the front door and moving toward his car with two framed photos in his hand.

— · —

Nancy Carli, who had been Nancy Darrow and was a teacher in the county school system, had dinner with her youngest son, Dean, that evening at six because her husband, Freddy, and the oldest boy, Nathan, would close the store and not be home until eight-thirty, and after dinner she called the store to talk to her husband.

Nathan answered the phone and spoke to his mother a while and then shouted, "Dad, it's Mom on two!" and Freddy picked up the phone. Their first words were distracted and ritu-alistic. "How's it going? Fine, you? Fine. Busy? Pretty good day. Need anything? Tomatoes…and ketchup," and then Nancy said, "Why were you home today?"

"Home?"

"Dean said you really freaked him out."

"I freaked him out?"

"Didn't you? He said he jumped five feet. Did he? I wish I could've seen that."

"When?"

"When you came home."

"When?"

"Will you stop this? You're messing with my poor tired brain."

"I'm just not understanding you."

"Okay. Why…did…you…come…home…today?"

"I didn't."

She paused. "He said you were home this afternoon when he was leaving."

"Nope."

"Why would he say that?"

"Wasn't home."

"Freddy."

"I wasn't home. He's fooling. He's bizarre. I have to help checkout. See ya."

"Why would he tell me that story?"

"I don't know. He's loopy. He's messing with your poor tired brain. Bye." But when Freddy cradled the phone, he thought suddenly of Walt Timmel and wondered why, and what the connection was, and then he remembered that Walt said he had seen him near the channel today, and he felt a mild confusion and a vague sense of alarm that had no form, and it dissolved as his right hand played the cash register like a piano.

—·—

FRED Carli hit the highway and drove out of town with the two framed photographs face-up on the passenger seat beside him. He drove until he saw a shopping mall and the tower of a chain hamburger restaurant, and he drove through and had his meal in his car in the wide parking lot, but afterward, when he walked toward the restaurant to use the bathroom, a car stopped near him, and a man shouted jovially, "So they let you out of that store sometimes," and Fred stood there and manufactured, screw by bolt by pulley, a smile that meant nothing. The jovial man said something about the Rotary and then asked Fred, "Like my new car?" Fred looked at the car and kept the smile and gave the man a nod. "What are you driving now?" the man asked him.

Fred wondered what to say, and then said the perfect thing. He said, "Rolls-Royce," and the man laughed and drove away laughing.

By seven-thirty Fred was parked down the road from the Tip Top Grocery, watching the doors, watching for himself to come out into the last of the daylight. By eight-fifteen, the clerks were leaving and the last of the cars pulling away from the store. Freddy had not come out. Fred drove around to the back of the store and stopped far down the alley where he could keep watch on a long, low station wagon parked near the loading dock, and he wondered what he would say as he left his car and moved toward the man who was himself and called out to him and faced him, faced the madness that was true and solid and made of stores and houses and children and photographs and fathers dead but not dead, but when Freddy Carli did walk out the back of the store, his older son was with him, and the two of them checked the locks and then walked to the station wagon, and Fred stayed in his convertible, his hands on the wheel, and didn't move.

— · —

FREDDY and the boy, Nathan, entered the wagon and Freddy backed up and drove away, heading for home, followed, at eight or nine car lengths, by a BMW which he didn't notice except as a pair of lights. He thought about dinner. He thought about what was on television that he liked to watch on Friday nights. He thought about Nathan beside him, stolid in his silence, as reticent as his brother was talkative, and he felt he should ask him something, and he asked, "You going out tonight?"

He then regretted asking because Nathan asked, "Why?"

And Freddy had to say, "Just asking," which was true, but sounded false.

"Don't know," Nathan said.

Freddy sighed and smiled at the road and said, "I just envy your energy, anybody's seventeen-year-old energy," saying that to soften the asking because Nathan was easily offended and would retreat into even deeper silences.

When they parked in the driveway of their home, Nathan was out first, grabbing the bag of tomatoes and ketchup and striding toward the door, and Freddy was slower, moving the heavy car door out of his way and giving it a shove to close it and stretching his back and then beginning to walk toward the porch, but he was startled and stopped by the insistent sound of a car horn, and he turned to see a small, sleek convertible parked nearby on the street, its lights on, motor running. As he glanced at it, the horn sounded again, and this time the sound entered him, like a chord of music and made him afraid, but he didn't know why. He turned to glance at Nathan, who was half in the door of the house and turning toward the convertible and then looking at Freddy. Freddy didn't say anything, but he half-raised a hand that was a kind of blessing, which translated as, "Go on, son, go into the house," and he started to turn toward the convertible, still glancing back until Nathan was inside, and then he walked on across his lawn to its bordering hedge, which was waist high, and he stared over this hedge into the driver's seat of the convertible just ten feet away.

Freddy saw himself seated behind the wheel of the convertible, met the eyes of himself and winced as if he had been slapped, and he stepped back, his face twisted by shock and by fear and by the sense of something terribly wrong, some awful mistake that was nearly impossible to look at but must be seen, must be studied, and he studied the face of himself that was also twisted and afraid but struggling against the fear, fighting so hard that the teeth were bared in an inner, torturous battle.

Freddy took one more step back, his mouth opening, and he saw tears come to the wide eyes that were staring at him from the car, giving him back his fear and some loss, too, some grieving loss for something, for a reality that was now broken and could never be repaired, and showing him the continuing struggle as the man in the car also opened his mouth, trying to speak to him, but the mouth wavered and shook and no words came, and the man, who was him, who was exactly him, suddenly faced forward in a wrenching panic and drove away.

Freddy watched the convertible pick up speed and turn recklessly at the corner, leaving behind only a diminishing sound and a memory that hammered at him and matched the hammering of his heart as he, too, felt the breakdown, the awful breaking down of the known world or the breaking down of his mind or maybe they were the same thing.

He watched the corner where the convertible had turned, watched the memory of it turning and passing out of sight, and he was afraid to look away. He should look away. He should look at his house. They were waiting for him in the house, but he was afraid to turn around and afraid to see his family and connect his family to this event that was some kind of awful breaking down, but he did turn, and his wife was there at the picture window, backlit by the glow of lamps, studying him where he stood in the yard.

The walk across the lawn to his house was the most difficult walk he had ever taken, and it was much too short because he had to change in just seventeen steps from a man who had walked off the earth and seen the void into a husband and father who was expected in the house.

"Who was it?" Nancy asked him.

He found himself hooking a word and dragging it up and out of him. "Somebody…"

She was waiting, and he was trying to rearrange his face into the usual face, into the husband coming home face. "I don't know."

"You don't know who was in that car?"

"Somebody…"

"They didn't say anything?"

"No. He drove away."

"But you don't know him?"

"I don't know." He was taking off his jacket because it was a normal thing to do, and she began walking ahead of him into the kitchen, and he followed, staring at the back of her, wanting to take hold of her and press her against him, but, instead, letting her walk on, innocent of the threat of this life-shaking chaos, not even knowing that she needed the protection he was desperate to give her.

"Why did he honk his horn like that?"

"I don't know."

"He didn't say anything? You walked over there, and he didn't say a word?"

"No."

"Strange," she said.

"Yes. Yes."

"Dad!" The youngest boy, always in hurried motion, flew into the kitchen and caught on the doorway, leaning in. "Tell Mom you were home today 'cause she thinks I'm making it up and messing with her brain."

Freddy stared at the boy, his mind rolling back to the

phone call from his wife, and rolling back further to his talk with Walt Timmel and then speeding forward to the man in the convertible, the man who was himself, the man who must have been near the channel talking to Walt today and then inside his home. Inside his home. He fought through shock and confusion and terror, moving as if through deep, sucking mud toward the boy who was waiting for him to speak, who needed him to speak and needed his protection from the terror so that the boy would not be touched by it and shaken by it as Walt had been shaken, and Freddy made himself say, "Yeah. I was home."

"See, Mom?"

"Why were you home?"

"Didn't…feel well…for a minute."

"Are you getting sick?"

"Just need to lie down."

"Why did you say you weren't home?"

"Didn't want to…worry you."

Gently, he fought off their concern, moving to lie in the dark bedroom with only the light from the hall spilling in, and he turned away the food that was offered, and he lay there on the bed, on top of the covers with his shoes off, and closed his eyes and saw the face of the man, which was his own, and then his wife came in after leaving him alone for half an hour and checked and saw that his eyes were open now, and so sat on the bed beside him.

He answered the question that her eyes asked him. "I'm all right," he said, and he wanted to weep because he didn't know if he would ever be all right, and he put a hand on her thigh and she covered it with her own, and he said "Lie down with me," and hoped he could keep her there without putting her in danger, without giving anything away, and she lay down facing him, and he touched her face and studied it, wondering, and he created a soft smile and moved his hand along her shoulder and down to her breast to rest there, and she lifted his hand and kissed it and put it back on her breast, and they stared, and he kept the smile in place and forced back the chaos roiling inside of him.

"Are you blue," she wondered softly, "or just brimming with sexual hunger?"

He managed his voice carefully and said, "Brimming," and the smile she made for him stood for everything, for all he treasured and wanted to keep, for everything that was now threatened.

"Hmm, I don't know," she said. "It's between you and this really good book I'm reading."

Inside he shouted, "God, I love us. I love us all, and I want…" But he felt tears in his throat and said only, "The book isn't real. But I'm real. Right? Am I real?"

She kept her smile, but a new thought overtook her, and she said, "Oh, did you move the photographs? Where are they—the one in the living room and the one here…of your father and the boys?" And he wondered how long he could protect his family from this thing, this thing he had seen face to face, this sickness, this man who was himself and had been inside his home, touching things, taking things.

"I was…looking at them. I put them somewhere."

"Today?"

They heard Nathan raise his voice in a kind of shouted mumble, "Going out."

Nancy said, "Wait," calling to the boy and leaving the bedroom, and Freddy was glad she was gone, but also wanted her terribly, wanted her in his arms, wanted to wake up from this, wake up and there would be a slash of sunlight on the carpet and Nancy breathing beside him and this would all be over.

— · —

FRED was driving too fast toward the motel, hoping his violent shuddering would stop so he could think. He pulled off the road and parked across three parking lanes in front of a liquor store and bought a bottle of vodka without saying a word. Five minutes more and he was in his motel room, a glass in his hand and the vodka carving through him like a blade as he stared at the telephone, needing to hear a voice from his life, from his own life, but not knowing who to call. If he called his daughter again, she would only think he was drunk, and it would be the same with his ex-wife. His girlfriend and he had parted and weren't speaking, and his friend, his best friend, Tim, was bitter now, because he had been let go from the company and Fred was still there, and Tim would only leak his bitterness into the call, and there was no one who would give him the voice he needed served without pain or guilt, so he drank again and stared at the phone, waiting to know who to call.

— · —

WHEN the telephone rang in Freddy's house, he swept his hand to the nightstand, beating everyone else in his family to the call because he knew, somehow, and his heart was suddenly punching him as he shouted through the walls, "I've got it!"

The phone was silent, and Freddy was afraid to be the one to begin this. He thought he heard breathing. "Who are you?" he asked, finally, and then his own voice came at him through the phone.

"Fred Carli."

"Jesus. Jesus," he said. "What's happening?!"

"I don't know." The voice on the phone sounded frightened, lost.

Freddy didn't know what to say, and then asked, suddenly, "Where did you come from?" his face tightening with a kind of revulsion as if he expected the answer to involve some infected cavern of his own mind.

Fred Carli, sitting on the bed of his motel room, said, simply, "Minnesota. Fucking Minnesota. For the reunion. You have to come here. Come here now."

And Freddy, in the darkened bedroom in his house, in the old house where both of these selves had grown up, said, "How can this be?"

"I don't know, but I think you have to come here and we have to see…how to end it. How to make it be over."

But Freddy was shaking his head, and he whispered, so that no one in the house could possibly hear him. "You're not real."

And Fred, in his motel room, whispered also, for no reason at all. "I am. Jesus, I am. Come here. Come to the Lake Motel on Renehan. I'm in room ten."

"Who?" Freddy hissed. "Who's in room ten? Who are you?"

"I'm as real as you are," Fred said. "I'm as real as you are," and then he hung up the phone with a trembling hand.

— · —

FREDDY put on his shoes and went into the living room and continued the battle that was the most difficult battle of his life, making every gesture and every word sound as normal as possible as the world was splitting, and massive structures of reality were caving in and crashing around him. He said this to his wife: "That guy in the car called, and I'm going to see him for a while. He's here for the reunion, and he wants to talk to me."

"Who?"

"I'm not sure."

"He won't say? You didn't recognize him?"

"I'm not sure."

"I'll get the yearbook. We'll find him. Wait."

"No. I'll be back in a while."

"You didn't eat."

"I'll be back in a while."

Freddy drove to the motel and parked and exited his car, all of his movements stiff and jerky, and he looked at the doors and saw number 10, and seeing the number rooted him to the spot where he stood.

— · —

FRED Carli, waiting in the motel room, poured himself his third glass of vodka and sipped it and walked around the room and into the bathroom and looked in the mirror and walked around again. The phone rang, and he answered it, and it was his own voice, saying, "I can't come in. I can't come in there."

"Where are you?"

"In the motel office. I can't walk in there."

"We have to... We have to!"

"Walk outside," Freddy said. "There's a field behind the motel. Walk out there. I'll walk out there now. I can't walk into that room." His voice shook, and it felt to him as if all the organs of his body were loose and moving and colliding. "I'll walk out there now," and he hung up the phone and walked out of the motel office and around the building into the field, which was dark beyond the motel lights.

Fred drank a full gulp of the vodka and squeezed his eyes closed and lowered the glass to the tabletop where it rattled before his hand left it. Then both his hands fingered through his hair, and he grabbed the key to his room, closing the key and the plastic tab in a tight fist in order to hurt his palm, in order to prove that he was awake and that he was real, and then he went outside.

— . —

FREDDY walked through the mostly barren, sparsely-weeded field, moving just past the rim of the lighted area where a thinned darkness took him in, and he felt safer there, less vulnerable than in a lighted motel room, enclosed by walls, shut in with...whom? With what? And he kept his eyes on the motel, waiting for a figure to detach from the building and come into the field, the figure of himself, and he shivered without being cold. He dug his shoes into the weeds and dirt to anchor himself, to test the reality of the moment, and he saw a shape moving in the darkness, and it was a dog, a short-haired dog, thin and quick, moving through the field at the rim of the light, and the animal looked at him as it moved on, and he studied it and realized that the dog had its own life and didn't know what was happening here and would never know and did not care. It was just moving through the rim of this impossibility and Freddy thought that when this night was over, and he was either dead or insane, the dog would still be moving on, still living its life, and then he looked away from the dog and saw himself coming through the field.

—.—

FRED left the protection of the building, his chest jumping with every breath, squinting past the parking lot lights, studying the field and seeing nothing, and then noticing, as the light thinned, a figure in the half-dark, the figure of himself, the self he had seen on the lawn of the old house, standing over the hedge of the old house, the same poplin jacket, the same shock and terror on the familiar face, except now, as he approached this self, he saw that the shock had melted into a kind of disgust, and this man, this self, looked away from him and stared at the ground and shook his head. Fred stopped just six feet from this other self who was called Freddy and had stayed, stayed in the old house, stayed in the old life.

—.—

THEY didn't speak at first. Freddy continued to shake his head, staring at the ground. Then he said, hoarsely, "I don't have a twin brother. This is crazy. You're not even here."

"You know I'm here. You know it."

But Freddy refused to look and turned to stare off into the deeper darkness. His eyes were wet, and he would not stop shaking his head. In a moment he swallowed, and, still staring at nothing, at the clouded night sky which looked like nothing, he said, "You were in my house. With my son! You were in my house."

"It's my house, too. It used to be."

"You took things… Jesus! I'm out here talking to nobody. How can I be talking to you? I'm talking to nobody, and somebody's going to see this and call the police and they'll take me to a mental hospital."

"Maybe they'll take *me*." And this made Freddy stop shaking his head and stare fully at Fred, the two of them studying each other and seeing themselves more clearly than any mirror or photograph had ever shown them.

"I have a picture in a frame," Fred said in a breaking voice, "that shows my father at least fifteen years older than he ever got to be. My father is dead! He drank himself to death years ago. He didn't get to be that old!"

"What world are you talking about?" Freddy was suddenly shouting, too. "What life are you talking about?"

"My life!"

"Not mine," Freddy said. "You're not me!"

"I used to be!" That stopped them both, saying it and

hearing it said, the impossible thing, the massive dark thought that was not believable, but stood there in front of them, and Fred swallowed, and he went on. "I used to live here. In that house. I used to be a boy here. I used to…"

"You couldn't because that can't happen. This is just some kind of sickness. I'm sick. You're…"

"I lived here! I remember it! I lived it all!"

"Lived what? Lived my life?" Freddy took a step closer, challenging. "You lived my life in Indian Lake?"

"Yes!"

"And took care of my sick mother…"

"With bleeding intestines, yes!"

"And put my drunken father to bed because she couldn't? Picked him up and dragged him and cleaned him since I was ten, and he fell on me…"

"And broke my wrist!" And Fred stepped closer to Freddy, pushing his arm at him, turning the hand to expose his wrist, the scar there, and Freddy looked at it, and looked at his own scar where the bone had come through the skin, the flat, white scar that identified him and even defined him, defined his early life, and it had a shape like a country on a map.

"India, I called it. We called it."

Freddy remained staring at his wrist and the shape of India there in scar tissue, and then he asked in a wet and rattled voice, "We?"

"When…you and I were… When we…"

"What? Were what?"

"Were one boy."

And they studied each other then, both their stares deep and wet and both their mouths unfirm, trembling, and Fred captured his mouth in his hand, and Freddy let two tears make a slow passage down his face to be lost in the bristles there, and he said, "There can't be two lives."

"We went to Minnesota."

"What?"

"Mom died, and Dad and I went to Minnesota. To her brother's place."

Freddy stared and then said, "Jeff. Uncle Jeff."

"Yes. She died, and he was drunk, drunk every day, every goddamn minute, and he didn't know what to do, and I said, 'Let's go, let's just get out of here. You always talk about selling the store. Sell it! Jeff says to come and work for him, live with him. Let's go!' She always wanted to go back. 'So let's go,' I said, 'let's just sell everything like you always said, and for once let's do something and let's go!'"

"No," Freddy said, remembering. "No, it's what I wanted to say. It's what I almost said."

"I said it!"

"No!"

"I said it! I grabbed him and I shook him, and I said it! I made him do it. I made him call everybody and get the papers and sign them and do it! And I finished college in Minnesota, and we lived there and got out of here forever, and we took her with us. We took her ashes..."

"She's buried! We buried her at St. Francis..."

"We took her ashes and got out and never came back..."

"I saw her buried!"

"We got the hell out of here!"

"I wanted to!"

"I did it! I got the hell out into the world, out of that house, that sick-house and that drunk-house and that store and this town and I got out!"

There was a long silence then, as each stared at the other and stared at the other life, the other unlived possibility, imagining it. "So you…" Freddy began. "You and Dad went away and never… And he died. You say, for you…he died."

"Yes. Yes, he died. The drinking killed him—twelve years ago. He never stopped. He…"

"He's alive. Sick but alive," Freddy said, quieter now. "Sober now, for years. He…comes in the store once a week or so, just to be…to be around, works a little."

"No, shit. Sober. Dad sober."

"Yeah."

"And you…married Nancy. Jesus." Fred was quiet also, busy imagining, remembering. "She was seeing Roger Kellen when I left, so… I figured that was over anyway, so…"

"She married him," Freddy said, realizing that they were sounding now like old friends, old friends at a reunion and not even mentioning the sickness, the tear in the world that was allowing this, but he went on anyway, telling it. "They had a son, Nathan. He's my stepson. We married later. Dean is ours. She's a teacher. And…you?"

"I'm an executive…at Pillsbury," and here Fred had the same thought, that he was making the talk he expected to be making at a reunion, but making now it to another version of himself in a dark field and somebody, or the world, was insane, but he went on telling it. "I travel a lot. My daughter just graduated college. I… Jesus Christ. Listen to me. Listen to us. This doesn't happen. This isn't allowed to happen."

"I know. I know." But Freddy wanted to hear more about his unlived life. He wasn't sure why, but he had to know. "You travel where?"

Fred shrugged, "All over for business. Overseas for… pleasure."

"You make a lot of money," Freddy said, and Fred shrugged again. "And you drive a nice car."

"I rented it. To show off. But yes… I drive a nice car."

"I wonder…" Freddy was staring very far off, overseas somewhere. "I wonder if I… Oh, Jesus," and he began to pace in the weedy field, his hand rubbing nervously at the back of his neck, and he was shaking his head again, his eyes wet again. "I almost said… Christ, I almost asked you, 'Did I ever get to Italy?' I almost said that. Shit. I can't stand this. What *is* this? *Why* is this?"

But Fred only stared at him for a long while, and then said, "Yes. Italy. A *Farewell to Arms*."

"Christ. Christ!" Freddy put both his hands on his head and kept walking about in the field. "I read it three times, and I wrote down all those towns…"

"I know. You think I don't know? That was me, too. That was me. Yeah, I went there. I saw them. I scratched them off the list. Milan. Bolzano…"

"And it was great," Freddy said, not asking, but knowing that it was. "It was great."

"Yes."

Freddy stopped walking then, and stared at Fred, at the self who had been to the northern towns of Italy, and the air went out of him, and his hands dropped to his sides. After a long moment, he asked, "What happens now?" And then he answered his own question. "You have to go away."

"Yes."

"You just go back where you came from, and it's over. You go back and you never come here again. Isn't that what happens?"

"I think so."

"So go." Freddy said this with an ache that broke his voice. "Just go."

"Yes."

"You're going?"

"Yes, but…"

"What? What!"

"I want to see him." Fred was discovering this, realizing it as he spoke. "Dad. I want to see…him now, the way he is now, here, alive. I want to see him…before I go." And that's why he came, he was thinking. That's the reason he had to come and was driven to come, the reason for everything, for the sickness and the wreckage of all the laws of possibility, so he could find what he left behind here, and it was his father, this version of his father, the father who had a chance and stopped the drinking before it killed him, this father who survived, and when Fred had seen that, he would have what he came for, and he would grow quiet inside and settle; he would settle and be able to live his life with some peace.

Freddy was staring and then began to nod, thinking it through. "He lives on his own. Little house in Indian Hill. You can…follow me there, and you can wait, and I'll knock and he'll come to the door and you can see him from your car. I'll talk to him in the doorway, and you can see him. And then you can go."

"No. No, I want to…be with him."

"You can't!"

"I just want a few minutes…."

"You can't! You'll make him crazy. You'll give him this craziness, this sickness, like you gave it to Walt, like you almost gave it to my boy…"

"I won't."

"You can't be with him!"

"He'll think I'm you! He'll just think I'm you." They both studied that possibility and said nothing, and then Fred went on. "I won't make him crazy. I won't say anything about…this. He'll just think I'm you," and after some silence, Fred said with more strength, "I need that."

"It's not safe."

"I need it. It's why I came here. I can see that now. Can't you see that? Look, I could do it without you, you know. I could stay here and find him and…see him on my own. He'll just think I'm you. For God's sake. You think I want to make him crazy?"

Freddy dropped his eyes to the weedy ground as if the problem was laid out there for him to study. "How do I know you won't?"

"Would *you*, would you make him crazy? I'm you, you know. For Christ' sake. I'm you."

Freddy studied his other self and the words that self had spoken, and he weighed them. "Why don't you pack your car, and then follow me to his house, and I'll give you five minutes, but you can't say anything, you can't slip, you can't make a mistake and make him crazy."

"I won't. I'll be careful. I just...want some time with him."

"Five minutes."

"Yes."

"Then you'll go forever."

"Yes."

— · —

FREDDY waited in his car where the motel parking lot met Renehan Road, the motor running but the radio quiet because he had so much to think about: his father soon to have a visitor from Minneapolis, from another life, from a split in the foundation of the world, and he was thinking about those northern Italian towns, too, and wondering if his other self had been there in the time of snow, and then the convertible was moving and coming up behind him, and he pulled out and led the way to Indian Hill and passed his father's house and stopped in front of an empty lot on the next block, and the convertible parked behind him.

They got out of their cars and kept to the darkness, flicking their glances at the lighted houses as if they were criminals or at least sinners, breaking the laws of nature. "Put this on," Freddy said, slipping off his poplin jacket and watching as Fred put it on and then inspecting his other self. "Better take off that fancy watch," he said, and Fred took off his watch and shoved it in a pocket, and Freddy looked at his own wedding ring. Fred didn't wear one. Freddy took off the plain gold band and handed it toward Fred, who reached out with his fingers to grasp it, but they both stopped and both shuddered with the same strong sense of something forbidden about one self touching the other, something dangerous and even grotesque.

Fred cupped his palm, and Freddy dropped the ring there and Fred slid it on. It fit. They studied each other for another moment. "You have my photographs," Freddy said. Fred hesitated, then stepped to his car, ducked in and came back to Freddy with the framed photos. He looked at them once more and handed them over. Freddy nodded and then said, "Get in."

They drove the block and a half in Freddy's station wagon like twin brothers and parked across the street from the small house where the window showed the blue light of a television screen. "You know how careful you have to be?"

Fred didn't speak, couldn't, staring at the house and feeling hollow, weak. He swallowed and opened the door, stepped out, closed the door quietly and looked briefly at his other self, and then walked across the street to the house. He could hear the television now, a comedy show with a laugh track, bursts of laughter that sounded like static. There were just two cement steps leading to the door. He was slowing. He stopped. He breathed with his mouth open, shuddering breaths, and then he forced himself forward. His shoes made gritty sounds on the cement, but the television was booming, the laugh track roaring, and then Fred heard, through the screen door, the laughter of his father, something impossible, and it held him still, not even breathing, but thinking, finally, that everything about this day was impossible. It was three repeated sounds of laughter, deep and rasping, and he stood outside the door, his mouth twisting, and he buried a sob in his chest.

He touched the handle of the screen door and paused. Knock or go in? Say something? He pressed down on the handle. The music of a commercial bounced up the volume and covered the sounds of the door swinging out and Fred slipping into the house. Just two steps would take him into the small living room, and he swallowed and took one and stopped. He could see the man in the chair, the side of him, long and bony, his feet in white socks resting on an ottoman. There was an oxygen tank near the chair, but not connected, and a medicinal smell and the smell of food, and the old man in the chair rubbed his chin and picked a piece of lint off his pants, and Fred watched every move with heightened focus, his mind screaming, this is him, this is him, and he didn't die, look at him; he didn't die. Then the old man became aware of a presence near the door and turned and his mouth opened in a gasp and he reared back in the chair and said, "Holy shit, you scared me. Jesus, Freddy. Jesus. You tryin' to give me an attack?"

Fred stared at the old man who was turned fully to him now

and was his father but not his father, no, not his father. He had
been his father long ago, but now was someone he didn't quite
know, and this revelation carved a hole in the center of him.
He could see his father in the man, but could see the rest of
him, too, the different part of him, all the years that this man
had lived in Indian Lake, lived here and not gone away, lived
here and thrived and sobered and stayed, and all of those years
made him into a man Fred didn't know.

"What're you doin'? What's wrong?"

He had to speak to this man. But this man didn't know him.
This man thought he was someone else.

"What's goin' on?"

"Nothing," Fred said, and he felt that, almost that, almost
nothing.

"Nothing? You look like hell. What's wrong? What're you
doin' here?"

He stared a moment more and then he said, "Looking for
you," and he said it simply, because it was true.

"Why?"

"To see…if you were still alive."

"Well, Christ. I'm still alive. What'd you think? Somebody
say I was dyin'?"

The long bony man who was clear-eyed, more clear-eyed
than his father and thinner, with a more shrunken face, and
with years, all those years on him, was waiting for Fred to speak
again, his old face squinting hard at who he thought was his
son, at who used to be his son long ago.

"You're alive," Fred said, and in his mind he added, but
you're not him. He was mine, my father, and you, old man, old

clear-eyed man, you belong to somebody else, and he felt the emptiness grow inside of him.

"I'm alive. No kiddin'. Hell, you oughta be a doctor. Do I owe you for this house call?"

"No."

"That's a relief. Sit down, for Christ sake."

"No."

"No?"

"I can't stay here." There's no one I know here, is what Fred would have added, but he had promised to keep this old man outside of the truth which would steal his reason, so he didn't say it.

"You were just drivin' by?"

"Yes."

"Everybody all right?"

"Yes."

"That's all you can say?"

Fred hesitated for one second and then said, "Goodbye, Dad," said it to the father hidden deep inside this old man, the father he had known as a boy and the father he had lost. He was afraid he would weep and frighten this old man, so he said, quickly, "Sorry I can't stay."

He turned and opened the screen door and left the house as the old man who used to be his father called out, "Come back and cheer me up again some time. Jesus."

— · —

Fred angled through the yard to the sidewalk, walking quickly, and he did not move toward the street where Freddy waited in the station wagon, but he walked and then jogged on toward his own car, his throat strangling from the inside and strange cries coming out of him and his eyes blurring with tears.

He entered his car and started it as his hand trembled and he turned on the headlights, and that's when the station wagon pulled up beside him, and Freddy was shouting at him, saying, "What are you doing? What did you say to him?" But he didn't answer; he pulled forward and surged out in front of the wagon and pressed on the gas and roared down the dark street and away.

—.—

FREDDY was stiff with terror, his limbs barely working as he turned the car into a driveway and backed up and sped back to his father's home. He parked and left his car and hurried toward the door of the small house, but stopped before he entered because his father was laughing, laughing at the television set as the recorded voices of a crowd surged and laughed with him, and then his father went on chuckling in raspy high notes, full of delight as the comedy continued, and Freddy took a step back from the door and then another and then walked to his car and drove home.

He pulled into the garage beside his house instead of leaving the wagon in the drive because he wanted the shelter. He wanted the moment alone in the silent garage, with the door coming down and closing him in and the killed motor still ticking and his thoughts able to settle, so that he could examine them, so that he could ready himself for his family and for their questions.

He walked through the front door and through the living room, remembering then that he didn't have his jacket, and then he clenched his left fist, remembering the ring. Fred had it, the other self, the self with the other life. Freddy kept walking, thinking of the lies he would tell, thinking of the man who was driving away now and would never come back, and maybe he would mail the ring to Freddy. No. There should be no more contact. Not even that. There must be nothing, forever. It had been a mistake, an error in the universe, a sickness in nature, like a virus, and it was gone now, and he would never forget, of course, but it was gone.

He walked into the dark bedroom and sat on the bed and pushed off his shoes and lay down, and then Nancy came in.

"So?"

"He wasn't there." The first lie. Freddy kept his left hand covered. "He didn't show up. I think he's crazy."

"No kidding. And you don't know who he is."

"No."

"I pulled out the yearbook. Shall we look?"

"Not now."

"Are you sick?"

He turned to her then, and she sat on the bed, and he was looking at her from far away, from another point in the universe, thinking what if he had gone away; what if he had never married her; what if he had said to his father what he couldn't say, said it and made his father leave the town and made himself leave, like he wanted to, many times, and make a different life, a larger life, a life of many places, a life that included the northern towns of Italy. Look at her. Look at his wife, Nancy, look at her looking at him, worried about him. Look at her, older now, a little thicker, a little more lined in the face, a little more gray in her hair as he was gray in his. Look at them, Freddy and Nancy, in their dark bedroom, in their life in Indian Lake.

"What's wrong?" she asked him, noticing that he looked at her deeply and from far away.

"My life is small," he said to her inside his mind, but aloud he said, "Nothing," the next lie.

"What're you thinking about?"

"I guess I'm thinking about that guy."

"What about him? He bothers you?"

"Yes."

"In what way?"

"Who is he?" Freddy asked aloud, but inside his mind he added, "And who am I?"

"We'll find him," she said. "In the book."

"Okay."

"You going to eat now?"

"No. Well maybe something. Just..."

"I'll heat the soup in case." And she leaned down and kissed his forehead, and he felt his love for her and his need for her fill him like a deep breath, and then she left the bed and left the room, and he watched her go.

In a moment he could hear her in the kitchen, an old familiar melody. He turned on the lamp and rose from the bed, walked to the closet and looked through his clothes to find the tweed jacket on a hanger draped in plastic, and he lifted the plastic and looked at it. He had bought it in London when the Rotary Club had gone over, eight families and all their kids, his one trip overseas. He had loved the visible history of the city, and he had loved the countryside and especially Scotland, the rugged, barren beauty of the highlands, and he had bought this jacket on the last day of the trip and paid too much.

It was called a shooting jacket, with a leather patch on one shoulder, and it fit him perfectly, and he had bought it because he had imagined himself wearing that jacket and coming back to Scotland, saw himself in the countryside without the Rotary, maybe without the kids, too, just him and Nancy. He had pictured himself in that jacket walking in the highlands of Scotland, and that's why he had bought it, and he ran his fingers over the soft tweed, deciding that he would wear this to the class reunion, deciding he would tell that to Nancy, and Nancy would say, "You'll be too warm in that," but he would wear it anyway, at least to walk in there, and wearing it would be like wearing the flag of another country, the colors of another land where he had been, where he would go again.

—·—

FRED Carli had driven away from the house of the man who used to be his father because he could not stay, could not look at that man, seeing his dead father hidden within the old body and the old face and the old eyes, the clear eyes that were not the dulled and not the shifting eyes of the father who had surrendered, had given in to the drink and killed himself in Minnesota just as if he had thrown himself into a river, except it was not a river and it had taken him years to drown himself, and Fred could not visit with that dead man who was hidden inside the old man in the chair, could not stand to remember watching him take the long, slow fall to his death, while Fred had thought, always thought, that there was nothing he could do, that the man was following his own will and his own fate and there was no other possible fate for him, and now Fred had seen the other possible fate, and he couldn't stand to see it anymore because it didn't belong to him, and it wasn't, after all, the reason he had come here.

There had to be another reason, something else to find, something in payment for all this sickness and fear, for the breakdown of all the machinery that was trusted to run and always run, forever, and it wasn't enough to see this other father, this father who had stayed and sobered and lived to get old. Good for him. Good for you, old man, but you're not my dad. My dad went to Minnesota and died in Minnesota, and I don't belong to you, and you're not enough in trade for all of this, so there's more. There has to be more.

And so Fred Carli was no longer driving away, but was on a hill then, pulled over to the side of a narrow road, and he could see the moon rising. He watched the sky for a while and the rooftops of Indian Lake as they were struck by the moonlight, and then he pushed at the door and got out of the car and opened the trunk and pulled out the bottle of vodka and opened the cap. He took a sip and then another, and then he downed a full shot and squeezed his eyes closed and breathed deeply as the alcohol rampaged through him, and then he put the bottle back where it was but changed his mind and drew it out swiftly with his left hand and threw it into the ditch. When he had grabbed the bottle, there had been a sharp clink that was caused by the wedding ring on his finger meeting the glass, and he stared now at his hand, at the gold band, as the moon eased upward. He realized, suddenly, that the gold ring and the poplin jacket were keys that could give him entrée anywhere in this town, anywhere in this life, and he felt their power, knowing that he could go to anyplace he wanted, now, at this moment, and he could be, for this moment, Freddy Carli, the grocer, the Indian Lake man, the man with the house on Idlewild Drive, and if anybody came to this hilltop now, anybody from any of the nearby towns, they would know him and they would call him Freddy and ask him what he was doing out here on this hilltop, and he would say, he suddenly knew what he would say, he would say, I was looking at the moon, and now I've seen it, and now I'm going home, home to my house on Idlewild Drive, and his caution was dissolved by desperation and by alcohol.

— . —

FREDDY was still holding the jacket, staring not at it but through it, when Nancy came into the room. She was carrying the Indian Lake yearbook of 1954, and he glanced at it, knowing that they would find no stranger there but only the photo of himself because he was still one person then and the world was whole. He put his eyes back on the jacket.

"Remember this?"

"Sure. You haven't worn that in… When?"

"I'll wear it tomorrow night."

"It's too heavy for the weather, Freddy."

A smile came to him then, without having to force or create it, and it felt good there on his face. "Listen," he said to her softly.

"What?"

He took a long breath, looking into her as she waited. "Do you think our life is small?"

"Small?"

"Yeah."

"Are you kidding? It's so big I can hardly carry it. Why would you think that?"

He shrugged and rehung the jacket and turned to her, and she was still staring at him, wondering. He said, "Let's go back to Scotland."

"Tonight?"

She had done it again, a sudden smile reshaping his face.

"All right," she said, "but first how about some soup?"

"A little later."

"Okay…then let's look at the yearbook, find this guy who's bothering you."

He could read her lingering worry and said, softly, "I'm all right, Nance."

"Good." She put her hand on his shoulder as they moved toward the door. "We'll make it an early night tonight. You can rest and I can get into this really good book I'm reading."

He laughed, remembering their talk earlier about making love tonight. It was just one short laugh, breaking quietly from his chest, but it was something he had thought, all through this day, that it might never happen to him again, a true laugh.

— . —

IN twenty minutes of Fred driving and losing his way and finding it again, he was back on the street where Freddy Carli lived a life that could have been his life, in a house that could have been his house, and he parked nearby and watched the lamplit windows, feeling his throat fill and knowing that if there was something for him here, something for him to find, some reason for the destruction of all the laws of life and time, it was in that house and in that light.

He noticed that there was no station wagon in the driveway, so he thought his other self was not there, his other self must still be with the old man who used to be his father, but Freddy's life was in there, in that house with the lamplit windows, waiting for him, waiting for Freddy to walk in the door, and Nancy was in there, Nancy Darrow, Nancy Carli now, inside and waiting for her husband to walk in, her husband in his poplin jacket and the wedding ring on his finger. All he had to do was walk to the door and open it and step in there, into that life. It was all waiting.

Fred eased out of the car and closed the door behind him with a soft click. He walked across the lawn, his quiet steps becoming louder, more brazen, let her hear him, he thought, let the light find him, so what? He was only Freddy now, walking toward his home, toward the door of his home, and he would step inside, deep inside the life there and find what he needed to find.

He reached the steps to the porch and took them and moved toward the door, wondering if it would be locked or if he would just turn and push and be inside the other life, and he was lifting his hands on the door handle and glancing into the picture window, where the lamps glowed, when he saw movement there.

He stopped and stared and then moved toward the window, one more step, two, and peered between the drawn shade and the window frame, and through that narrow separation he could see a woman's legs beneath a skirt, a woman seated on a sofa, and he took one more step closer and there she was, the woman who had been a girl when he had kissed her and held her and loosened her clothes and she had made fists in his hair and they had clung and ached and put their mouths together for the very breath of life, and there she was as she was now, and he moved even closer to the slim opening of the shade and saw that Nancy Carli was sitting beside her husband, Freddy Carli, and they were looking at a book, and Nancy was turning the pages, and Freddy was mostly silent and staring at the pages, but Nancy was animated and smiling and speaking, and Fred, outside, could not hear the words, but he watched them on the sofa, watched their faces, watched Nancy beside his other self, the self who had stayed, watched them and watched them.

There were two moths scribbling in the air outside the window, attracted by the lamplight, and a warm night wind that was hissing in the shrubs, and there was Fred studying intently as Nancy turned the pages and the man who could have been him sat beside her and now smiled slowly, softly at something she said, and she laughed and pointed to the page, and Fred studied them in their life, in the life they belonged to, and he felt a great space inside of him that was absent everything except an unnamed longing, just longing itself, moist and palpable and unnamed, and he swallowed and retreated from the window, step by careful step, and he slipped off the poplin jacket and removed from a pocket his expensive watch, which he slid onto his wrist, and then he slipped the wedding band from his finger and put the ring in the pocket and laid the jacket over the wrought-iron railing of the porch, and he turned and walked across the dark lawn before the moon rose high enough to find him.

He crossed the yard toward his car, realizing he was leaving all over again. He was running away again, and the truth came and settled into that empty space inside of him, the truth that in all the running, in the first running and in the constant running, he had been running away from himself.

He drove toward Chicago, thinking through the maze of highways that would get him to the airport, but he didn't want to go home, and he discovered where he wanted to go, the only place he wanted to go. He would fly to Ann Arbor again and knock on his daughter's door. Or should he call first? He didn't want to say on the phone what he wanted to tell her, what he was thinking over and over and reshaping in his mind in the car—that she shouldn't worry, because he wouldn't crowd her. He didn't want to crowd her or to push himself at her, but just to stand there at her door, clear-eyed, and tell her that he knew that it was her that he had lost along the way, and that he was sorry, and that he would be there for her if she ever needed him, not there for the little girl he had lost, but for the young woman he might be able to befriend, the young woman he admired because she was creating her own life now, and he would create one, too, in a new place. He would start again somewhere and find a job and meet people and find a place to live and find a life, the beginning of a life he might belong to.

— · —

FREDDY Carli was parking his station wagon and walking across a dirt road at 7:45 the next morning, the day already warming as he crossed the dusty street and moved toward a small house that had been beaten nearly to death by the weather and flayed by time and neglect. He mounted the cracked boards of the stairs and knocked on the screen door without hesitation. He knocked again.

A tall man came out of the gloom and moved toward the door and the light of the morning. He was carrying a nearly empty bottle of beer and he was dressed in yesterday's mussed and wrinkled clothes. The man stared at Freddy with sodden eyes that focused and gave way and focused again, and the eyes were full of anger and fear.

"Sorry to come so early, Walt," Freddy said, and the man's expression made no change. "I just wanted to say that I'm sorry about yesterday."

Those words froze the tall man, all his fear and anger still there, but suddenly on pause. He was not breathing.

"I'm sorry I played that trick on you down by the channel."

The long face moved then, slowly, and the eyes began to change, not only softening, but moving toward tears, and the expression that was being built second by second beyond the screen door was shaping itself toward a bottomless joy.

"All that stuff I said about Pillsbury."

Walt touched the inner handle of the screen door, pressed it down, began to open the door, so that Freddy took a step back and down to a lower stair, and all the while Walt was working on his growing smile, his eyes fully tearing now. He kept coming, without moving his stare, slowly coming outside as Freddy backed another step and another, with Walt looking like a man in a painting now, an old painting, the face of a saint struck by a holy light. He said, "Pillsbury," just to hear the word, and Freddy nodded.

"Yeah, a guy I knew visited me, and he had this car I thought was cool and he said 'go ahead, drive it around, pretend you're me.' Just kidding, but I...sort of did that, you know, like I was the guy from Minneapolis and..."

"Minneapolis, Minnesota," Walt said, his steps bringing him very close to Freddy now and his tears coming and his smile still spreading both wide and deep.

"So I shouldn't've tricked you..."

"Full beard," Walt said, as if it were a punch line, laughing a bit here, while his jaw shook with the soft weeping.

"Yeah, growing it, but then I said hell with it, and shaved it off. So...sorry again."

Walt was nodding and weeping and smiling all at once.

"So, buddy—gotta go open the store now."

All of Walt's motions continued as Freddy took a few steps back, and now the tall man did not follow.

"See ya later, Walt." Freddy turned and walked across the road to his car, entered and started the engine. He glanced, just enough to see that Walt was still in place, still smiling, and now beginning to raise a hand, the one with the beer bottle in it, in a gesture of farewell.

Freddy waved and pulled onto the road and drove on, pouring out a mighty sigh that emptied his chest and was a kind of period, a finishing of something as he sped toward his store and his life, and in his rearview mirror he saw Walt Timmel's smile following him like a bright and fervent light.

— . —

About the Author

Gerald DiPego is a writer of fiction in all forms, including the novels *Cheevey* (a top pick of the New England Independent Booksellers Association), *With a Vengeance* (critically acclaimed by *The New York Times*), *Keeper of the City* (adapted as a movie for *Showtime*), and others. He's written many short stories and stage plays, and his play *154 and Paradise* has been produced at Santa Barbara's Center Stage to sold-out audiences. He has also published a how-to book for aspiring writers: *Write! Find the Truth in Your Fiction.*

He has written screenplays for over thirty movies including *Sharky's Machine, Phenomenon, Message in a Bottle, Angel Eyes, Instinct, The Forgotten, and Words & Pictures.* He was twice nominated for the Writers Guild of America screenwriting award. Among his films for television, *A Family Upside Down* won a Golden Globe award as best picture, and *I Heard the Owl Call My Name* appeared in *Great Television Plays Vol. 2*. His screenplays have attracted top talent including Paul Newman, John Travolta, Anthony Hopkins, Juliette Binoche, Clive Owen, Kevin Costner, Jennifer Lopez, and Robin Wright.

DiPego lives and writes in the Santa Ynez Valley of California.

www.geralddipego.com

Printed in the USA
CPSIA information can be obtained
at www.ICGtesting.com
LVHW051117090324
773806LV00001B/139

9 798989 122707